and the
Alaskan
BEARS

The fifth book of the Alaskan Adventure Series

by
Bill Richardson

The Alaskan Adventure Series can be read in any order.

And there isn't any sex, cussing, or violence in the books!

All the characters in the stories are composites of people I knew personally or was involved with.

The Alaska information is accurate.

The books are based on my personal adventures as a former pilot, survival instructor, search and rescue navigator, teacher, outdoorsman, sailor, and so on!

I experienced most of these bear events!

Other books by Bill Richardson:

First: "Corky's Courage, An Alaskan Adventure"
A survival story after an airplane crash. The book is now being used as a survival guide.

Second: "Corky and the Alaskan Oldtimer"
An Alaskan Adventure Mystery novel concerning Nels, the gold miner!

Third: "Corky and the Alaskan Quake"
A Suspense novel of happenings before, during and after the Big Quake.

Fourth: "Corky and the Alaskan Gold Digger"
A Suspense novel of post earthquake emergency support and gold prospecting.

My books are also available as e-books.

My thanks go to Rene', Noralee, and others for their contributions to and for the Alaskan Adventure Series.

This is a work of fiction and therefore the names and any resemblances to persons, living or dead, or to any business, or aircraft numbers are entirely coincidental.

I'm solely responsible for the contents in this novel.

Copyright 2016 by William C. "Bill" Richardson

All rights reserved including any images.

No part of this book may be reproduced, scanned, or distributed in any printed or electronic form without permission.

First Edition: Aug., 2016

Printed in the United States of America

ISBN: 978-0-9969864-7-2

Table of Contents

CHAPTER 1 THE GOLD FINDERS ----------------------------- 5
CHAPTER 2 THE VISITORS -------------------------------- 14
CHAPTER 3 THE RED FOX --------------------------------- 23
CHAPTER 4 SWEET CINNAMON ROLLS ----------------------- 26
CHAPTER 5 THE SKUNK CABBAGE BEAR -------------------- 29
CHAPTER 6 SELDOVIA ------------------------------------ 36
CHAPTER 7 SIXMILE LAKE BROWNIE ----------------------- 43
CHAPTER 8 PAM --- 47
CHAPTER 9 THE DECISION -------------------------------- 53
CHAPTER 10 NORTH FORK VISITOR ------------------------ 65
CHAPTER 11 MACLAREN RIVER ---------------------------- 70
CHAPTER 12 SKILAK LAKE FOLLOWER ---------------------- 74
CHAPTER 13 DANE'S ENCOUNTERS ------------------------- 83
CHAPTER 14 NAKNEK SURPRISE --------------------------- 89
CHAPTER 15 COOPER LANDING ---------------------------- 94
CHAPTER 16 GLACIER BAY ------------------------------- 98
CHAPTER 17 KLAWOCK RIVER ---------------------------- 101
GLOSSARY --- 106

Chapter 1   The Gold Finders

Using a set of tweezers, Marian put the fourteen gold flakes one by one into a small glass vial containing a small amount of water. The small flakes didn't always fall off the tweezers so they were swished off with the water. In a few minutes the last of the gold was in the vial and the cap was twisted on tight. The small vial was then put into a soft leather poke bag. After the top strings were pulled tight, it was set into her backpack.

To be sure their prospecting activities would be kept up to date, Marian pulled out a small weatherproof field book. With a pencil she wrote in the date and the spot where they found the gold which was at the first Cross on Nels' plat map. She also wrote in the weather condition at the time they had been digging and the type of work each person had performed. The last entry was how much and what type of gold had been recovered.

Meanwhile, Bobby and Carver were packing up the prospecting gear for the next hike. The shaker box was taken apart and again tied to Carver's pack with his gold pan latched to the outside so it would be easy to get off. With the use of Marian's pan two people could do a quick survey of a likely site.

Carver was using a shovel as a walking stick and in a few minutes he was standing with the pack on and was ready to look for more gold.

Bobby reloaded his own pack with some of the food and water from Marian's so she wouldn't be carrying so much weight. The additional load on Mark's pack meant he had to reset the picks a little higher from where they had been so the extra weight wouldn't be trying to pull him backwards.

Marian finished the paperwork, adjusted the contents of her bundle, and then opened up their map before she lifted her pack onto her shoulders.

"Okay fellows, here's the next cross on the map. No doubt the creek has changed its course a little bit so let's keep an eye out for any other likely spots for a test pan.

"Are we ready?"

"I'm ready to do some more digging," Carver stated with excitement and a grin. "That was fun and easy."

Bobby nodded in agreement while he adjusted the shoulder straps on his pack. "Yep, this was an easy one, but I'm sure we have lots of work ahead of us. And until we learn how to really prospect an area we'll be putting in more work than we will later for the same results.

"Well then, off we go. I'll take the lead for a distance and if we find a good camping spot we should set it up and explore from there."

Slowly, and carefully, Bobby headed down the gravel bar to the creek bank. While using his shovel for support, he stepped up onto the higher ground and turned to help Marian. However, she had already moved up behind him so Bobby moved ahead to get out of her way.

With a hand outstretched Carver reached up to grab Marian's. "Grab me by the wrist and I'll grab yours. That way we get better grip. If we just use our hands we can slip, or worse, pull some finger muscles."

"Makes sense to me Marian," Carver replied as he wrapped his fingers around her wrist as she did the same for him. "Let's do it!"

With a smooth combined effort Carver and his heavy load were off the gravel bar and on the trail.

"Notice if you will that I was too close behind Bobby when I got up here. If he had turned around at the wrong time we would have bumped into each other and I would probably have fallen. I should've waited for him to have moved farther down the trail or to let him help me.

"Give the person in front of you plenty of room to maneuver. And always stay far enough apart that you can see and talk with them. Sometimes you need to let a companion know about a bear, or some type of danger, or whatever."

"Thanks for the tip. I haven't had much experience hiking with others. Nels and I spent time together, but not for more than a few days and that man could walk faster than anybody I've ever seen."

"That's what I've heard," Marian remarked as she turned and headed out to follow Bobby who was a few yards away. Soon the three were hiking along the trail that was marked on the map and that had been used by Nels' to get to his claims.

As they moved along they all chatted about how the spring season had reached their country. The snow was melting and the trail was getting mushy. The willows had that pre-growth yellowish brown cast to the branches. Occasionally, a little brown bird would fly so quickly past them it couldn't be identified.

"Bobby," Marian said urgently, but quietly. "Look off to your right! Is that a big Raven's head poking above the dry grass just on top of that rise a hundred yards away? I think it's watching us."

"I see it. It sure does seem to be checking us out. It looks at us, and then rotates its head downstream."

Carver had moved close to Marian when he stated, "Nels said to always follow what the Raven is telling you!"

Marian wanted to snap her head around in surprise, but didn't. Very slowly, she turned and in a hushed voice while looking directly into his eyes, replied, "Nels a smart man. He told you a powerful thing about the Raven."

Carver didn't move as he responded to her, "I've always felt Nels knew more about Alaska's pulse and spirit than many of the people who live here, and you folks respect that. That's one reason I've wanted to be with you people."

"That be good. Remember we just small part of this bigness. Bobby feel same. Stay true to that and you have a great life." She softly touched his arm, and then turned away when tears started to fall down the lad's cheeks.

Bobby didn't hear the words between his wife and their friend, but he saw that something serious and tender had just occurred. With a real sense of pride he nodded at the Raven, and then started to walk on the trail downstream and farther into the gold country.

The Raven flew off and seemed to be heading in the same direction as the prospectors.

Every step was carefully taken to avoid a deep mud hole, or to prevent a boot from sliding off one of the small hummocks that could injure an ankle, or break a leg.

The trail was a few yards from the stream bed and occasionally it seemed to move away from the water for no apparent reason. When the three weren't sidestepping a mud hole or missing a tripper of some kind they kept an eye out for a likely gold-bearing gravel bar.

After they had slogged along for another mile Bobby stopped at an area where the main creek was making an almost ninety degree turn away from their path.

He turned completely around to face the others, and then pointed to his left while asking, "What do you think about setting up camp on that rise over there?"

Then he pointed the opposite way and asked, "And then we do a test dig over there?"

Marian and Carver grunted something in response as the three worked their way over to the knoll that had a few small Cottonwood trees close a thick Alder grove. It would provide some wind protection, dry firewood, and enough flat ground for a decent camp.

After helping each other take off their packs they set to work making a siwash camp. Bobby and Carver strung a rope about five feet above the ground and attached it to a couple of nearby Cottonwood trees. Instead of setting up the tent they laid it under the rope, and then back over the rope so it stuck out about six feet at a slight upward angle from the taut cross rope to form a pitched roof.

The bottom corners were tied to some Alder bushes. The back portion of the tent was held in place by a thick alder log that was rolled inside and up against the fold. Now the cover wouldn't be able to flap from the wind.

Meanwhile, Marian cleared away the grass and twigs for a fire spot about three feet from where they would be sleeping. With a fire in the cleared area they would get heat from it while the lean-to gave them good protection from rain and even a strong wind. If the wind blew smoke into the lean-to it usually wasn't an issue for more than a few seconds.

The three picked up as much of the dry grass as they could find. Every blade was spread out between the fire pit and the back wall to create a dry boundary between the ground and the sleepers. The layer of grass would help to keep the cold ground from stealing heat from their bodies which could cause hypothermia.

A light tarp that was large enough for them to be able lie down side by side was then spread over the grass. All three of the prospectors would now be sleeping with their feet close to the fire while being covered by the overhead tent. Any light wind or rain that might occur would only be a minor disturbance.

After everyone had set their rolled up sleeping bags on the tarp they stood back and surveyed their work.

"Nice camp fellas! We be comfortable," Marian stated while surveying the setup. Then she patted her stomach and added, "Shall we eat before checking the creek? I'm sure hungry."

"I can always eat something," Carver exclaimed. "How can I help?"

"Food sounds good Mrs. Randall," Bobby said with a twinkle in his eyes.

"You boys collect wood. I build fire. Get out the food. We eat lots!" Marian declared in 'short talk'.

The two men quickly spread out to the Alder patches and Cottonwood trees to get dry firewood.

Almost immediately, Carver called out from about five feet from a Devil's Club patch.

"Bobby! Marian! Come take a look at this! I think these are fresh bear tracks from one smart bear. It's gone around all those branches of that Devil's Club bush. I know from experience how painfully vicious those spines can be.

"I got hit by them big time. They punctured my hand and arm and leg. It seemed to take forever before every mean needle of that stuff worked its way out of my skin. Could be this bear has had that same experience."

Bobby had his hand on his holstered pistol as he and Marian rushed over to join Carver who kept pointing at the ground by his boots.

Several fresh tracks that were about the eight or nine inches across were showing in the mix of slushy mud and snow. The bear had been walking around the base of the hill and on the outside of the Alder and Devil's Club patch instead of inside the thicket.

"I'm not certain Bobby, but I think these are black bear tracks. I've seen some like these when the blackies have been around our house, or by the river where I was fishing for salmon."

"You're right Carver. The blackie's tracks are pretty easy to recognize as the back toes are in a definite curve and a brown bear's are usually in a straight line.

"Notice how the back foot pad is shaped like a tear drop. In a grizzly or brown bear, it is typically in a long triangular shape, not always though.

"And over there are two front prints. Those toe pads are in a definite arc. A brownie's are typically in a straight pattern, and again, not always."

Marian nodded her head as Bobby explained about the tracks and when he had stopped she added, "Yep. Good black bear tracks. Nice find Carver. Just remember you can easily mistake a blackie's or brownie's tracks in the grass or moss. The bear belongs here and always be respectful to them. We don't want to disturb them. We always keep an eye out in case they want to visit us!"

"No problem, Marian. With this warm Spring weather we might be seeing more bears: browns and/or blacks. This one went down this hill into that creek bottom."

Marian nodded her head before stating, "If you spot or smell any Skunk Cabbage be sure to look for bears as they like to eat that when they come out of their den. It cleans out their stomach system so they can start eating again. A bear must like the rotten smell of that Skunk Cabbage. To me I call it 'Stink Weed'."

Marian checked the surrounding area to see if a bear was in sight before she looked back at her companions and directed, "Hey! Bear Watchers! I need lots more of that firewood if you want to eat tonight. I'm going back to the camp. I get my food ready to eat."

The two men quickly started picking up any kind of dry wood they could reach as she turned, and with a chuckle, headed back to the nearby camp to start a small fire and prepare their meal.

After a few minutes the wood gatherers had arrived with armfuls of firewood, and then neatly laid it by the ground tarp in two stacks.

One stack consisted of small dry twigs and sticks used to start a fire or make it burn hotter and fast. The other pile had several small dry logs that were about the thickness of a person's wrist, but two or three feet long. The piles would be easy to reach to keep the fire going at night to ward off the chill.

There was an added benefit to having the fire: most animals, including bears, won't get close to a campfire.

A covered metal pot sitting on a rock next to the fire was filled with English Breakfast tea.

Placed nearby were a metal tablespoon and a round flat yellow can filled with sugar. The can's label read "Darigold Butter".

Marian was setting the wrapped sandwiches next to three empty cups as the crew finished with the wood gathering, and then hunkered down by the small fire.

"Okay fellas, the sandwiches are made with corned beef and homemade bread. I think Glenda had put spicy German mustard on them. The thermos will be opened tonight to drink later when the fire has gone down.

"After we eat and check the creek maybe we should just camp here for the night. We've had a long walk and a good workout for our first day.

"What do you guys think about that idea?"

Bobby was the first to respond as he poured hot tea into a cup, "I was wondering about that same notion. We have had a great start and we don't need 'The Digger' to get worn out!"

"Oh, it'll take more than one dig to wear me out Mr. and Mrs. Randall," Carver said while flexing both of his arms. "I've just begun to dig!"

The three laughed and chatted as they removed the wax-paper from the sandwiches and started eating.

Chapter 2   The Visitors

The sun was close to the horizon by the time the three had worked their way through the Willow bushes to a steep creek bank. Soon they were helping each other climb down to a long gravel bar that curved out about fifteen feet into the stream and was forty feet long.

"Look here," Marian said excitedly as she pointed to a sandy patch. "Aren't those wolf tracks?"

Bobby and Carver looked at the area where she had kneeled down to inspect the animal sign.

"Nope! I think a Moose made these," Bobby stated. "And I see only two blurred prints here in the sand before the animal walked on the gravel and headed downstream."

Bobby walked where he thought the Fox had been before he pointed down, and then up towards the bank. "Here's where it might have jumped up into the Willows."

"Why do you think it wasn't a wolf Marian?" Carver asked as came back from the water's edge to look at the prints by her feet.

"A wolf and fox have similar tracks Carver. The wolf has a larger paw print that is about a third longer than it is wide. The four long front oval pads sit ahead of a squatty pyramid pad and usually you can see all four nail marks. These two tracks are almost as long as they are wide and two nail marks show at the very top. The four front pads are quite round and so is the bottom pad. I'm not real positive, but just from their size and general shape they are Fox prints. The Coyote would have four triangle front pads and a triangle base."

"And these tracks where the animal jumped are like a Fox's tracks," Bobby added as he lifted his hands into the air mimicking the fox jumping up and onto the bank.

In a smooth motion Bobby turned and pointed to the lower end of the bar before he commented, "Also notice the sand has piled up downstream at this end of the bar. If you look the upstream there are rocks at the end. From what Jeff said these are signs there could be some gold on the upstream end as the heavy stuff falls out first.

"In this case maybe the heavy stuff is only the rocks. Since we did find gold farther upstream I think we have a good chance of finding some here."

Marian was nodding her head in agreement as she surveyed the spots Bobby was describing.

"Wellllll," Carver drawled in a long breath. "We would want to set up our shaker on the upstream end of the bar the first thing in the morning!"

Bobby had walked over to the others while he was moving his hand from the downstream to the upstream area as he explained, "That would seem to be the logical thing to do except the creek level might go down during the night. The day's warm air melts more snow into water that then flows into the creek. And the water might even expand from getting warmed up on its run over a long stretch if there isn't a lot of cold water feeding into it.

"At night the temperature goes down and if it's low enough the water shrinks up and the level will go down.

"Since we have a small shaker we can move it as we need to if the water rises up pretty fast."

Carver, who had been listening closely then added, "What if we set the shaker out here in the middle of the bar and we dig a few test holes first. We can do them along its width and breadth. As we find a hot spot we'll just take the shaker to it, or wait until we've surveyed the whole bar, and then work the good test spots."

Marian chuckled and the two men looked at each other, and then back at her.

"What are you chuckling about Miss Sweetie?" Bobby asked his wife.

"We're such beginners," Marian said before giggling again, "and we don't have a problem trying to figure out what and how to finish the next challenge that comes up. I've met people who would run away so fast from the idea of even having so much work ahead of them."

"Not me!" Carver said as he did a quick two-step jig.

Bobby just kept moving his head up and down like a chicken as he replied back, "I wouldn't know what to do with myself if I didn't have a list of work to do."

"Okay. If we are all in agreement we'll bring the shaker and tools down tomorrow morning, do some test holes, record the good and the bad, and maybe do some test shaking."

Carver waved his arms up high over his head as he shook his hands. Then his shoulders shook. Then his chest and down to his hips and his feet.

"Just a test shake to get the gold settled into the bottom of my pockets!" he called out.

Marian quickly moved next to the young lad and both of them began yelling out screeches and bellows as they danced the length of the bar.

Bobby laughed and started clapping in the rhythm of a Jewish dance.

In a few moments they had stopped and were bursting with laughter just as a Super Cub on skis flew over them.

The three dancers ducked down as Bobby asked, "Where did that come from?"

"That's Eight-one-charlie! Corky's Super Cub! And she's circling and coming back," Marian said. "No doubt she'll think we've been overcome with gold fever!"

The Super Cub flashed its landing light at the three before it turned ninety degrees to the right of the three and headed behind the knoll where the camp had been set up.

They all decided to stay on the bar until they knew what Corky's intentions were.

In a few minutes the Cub came back to circle the three as someone waved from the backseat.

"It's Mom," Bobby called out as the three gave a hearty wave back.

The Cub circled, and then slowed down a little before it again flew back past the camp.

In a few minutes the aircraft had come back, made a reverse turn and with the flaps extended completely, it dragged itself back over the bar and the campsite.

"She's going to land on that knoll above the camp," Marian and Bobby said at the same time. Quickly, the three headed to the bank to get off the stream bar.

As they moved along they heard the sound of the plane's engine almost disappear, and then suddenly a very loud rush of power.

The sound caused Carver to get a concerned look so Marian pointed out, ""That's Corky doing a 180 degree turn at the end of her landing so she can travel back on the same tracks she just created. The power will be kept on while taxiing back to this end.

"However, our Miss Corky is using wheel skis. Did you notice the skis were jacked down so the bottom of the tire was barely showing? The skis will get pumped up after she lands and turns around or after she has taxied back to her starting point. With the skis partway down part of the tires will be touching the snow. Of course if the snow is packed hard enough the plane won't sink into it.

"If the snow isn't deep enough she'll pump the skis up a little so the tires make as good a contact with the brush and ground as possible.

"And after stopping, if she doesn't pump up the skis, she'll climb out and put a baseball bat under each ski to keep it from freezing into the snow. The skis can get warm from sliding so they melt the snow or ice. The melt water freezes, the skis will stick to the ice. If you don't put a stick under them right away you can spend hours getting freed up again.

"And that last engine roar is to turn the plane around on this end so it is headed in the direction she wants for her takeoff."

While the three waited at the camp for Corky and Paula to show up, Marian put another stick of wood on the fire as Carver just kept looking in the direction of where the plane had landed.

Bobby had just wiped out his and Marian's cups so the two guests could have some hot tea when they heard a voice call out, "Hello the camp!"

Carver snapped his head to his left towards the sound when he realized the ladies had walked along the sunny side of the hill and not over the top like he had thought they would.

Bobby and Marian quickly moved over the mix of snow and moss to greet their visitors with hugs and lots of laughter.

Carver stood still by the fire in total silence as Corky approached him with her hand extended to shake his.

"Hi Carver! It's nice to see you again. I hear you're quite the gold digger!"

A big smile crossed the lad's face before he responded and shook her hand, "I really enjoy doing it. How are you, Corky? I watched you fly in."

"This is interesting. First of all he didn't leave the camp to greet us, which is certainly okay. However, he didn't say anything until I spoke first and yet his response is friendly enough. I wonder what goes on in his mind."

"I'm fine, Carver. Paula and I thought we'd drop by for just a few minutes and say 'hi' to you three."

Paula walked over to the pair and extended her arms to hug Carver. "You're looking good Mr. Digger! Like maybe you're having some fun!"

Carver smiled again and quickly hugged her. "It has been fun. We're going to test that gravel bar down there in the morning," he stated before adding, "Oh, the corned beef sandwiches you made sure were good."

"I'm glad you liked it," Paula responded as the five gathered around the campfire. "We're staying for just a few minutes. Corky wants to take off before the sun goes down completely."

Marian was handing each of the visitors a cup of tea poured from the Thermos bottle as Corky added, "Mark and I landed our Cubs on that open muskeg just south of the cabin.

"Mark wanted a nap and Brenda is baking bread so Paula and I decided to fly up here to see where you folks would be, and maybe stop to say hello if we did find a good landing spot."

Paula had sipped some tea before she followed up on Corky's comments. "You sure made great progress today by getting this far."

"Yeah, especially for a bunch of beginners," Bobby said with a grin. "And we even discovered some gold!"

"You did?" Corky and Paula chimed out together. "Can we see it?"

Marian had already pulled out the vial with the gold flakes from her pack to show the guests and as she gave it to Corky she commented, "We are constantly working on our method of where to find potential gold sites, how to use the gold pans to test an area, who works best with the different tasks, and so on and on. We haven't moved up the creek very fast, but then that's not our objective. This is a survey trip and so far we've accomplished a lot."

"You sure have." Corky said. "It's sure exciting to see these flakes. Speaking of flakes, I have a question for all of you," Corky said with a serious tone, and then smiled as she asked, "What was all the jumping about on the gravel bar a while ago?"

A sudden chorus of laughs and smiles popped out of the three prospectors as they made more whooping noises and jumped around the visitors.

In a few moments they stopped, and with a solid grin on her face Marian explained, "We were just all shook up about what we might find with a few test holes. Just us being silly!"

"Carver is sure comfortable with Bobby and Marian. Once he breaks loose from being so quiet and withdrawn he can be a real hoot!"

"Wow! I'm relieved," Paula quipped. "I was afraid the German Mustard was too strong!"

"Oh, that was good mustard, Paula. Hopefully, no bear has smelled it," Carver noted as he waved to Corky and Paula to follow him over to the bear tracks by the Devils Club.

Corky kneeled down and examined the prints before stating, "It looks like a small black bear has been through here. Probably yesterday."

"And that's what we thought," Bobby stated. "And over there on the bar we found some Fox tracks. This is animal country and with this warm break-up weather we might be seeing a lot more tracks and animals."

"I didn't see any tracks on our way from the plane, which we need to get back to before we lose our daylight.

"You folks are doing great. Need anything before we leave the lake tomorrow?"

The trio looked at each other and without a word they shrugged their shoulders.

"Okay, we're out of here! Thanks to you all for doing such a great job. We'll be sure to tell Mark and Brenda where you are and what you've found and they'll be real excited too," Corky stated as she and Paula set their empty tea cups by the fire. "And you don't need to walk to the plane with us, so let's say goodbye from here."

"Hopefully, my attorney has sent the gold camp share agreement to my Homer address. I don't want

anyone upset about their pay and what share of the gold they will get, or not get. Gold sharing problems have a long history in and out of Alaska's gold camps. We sure don't need any discontent at this one."

As they started to leave Paula remarked, "I meant to tell you folks that we found Wolf tracks by the lake right when we got back from starting out with you this morning. There seems to have been two or maybe three animals. Those tracks weren't down there earlier when we pulled out our buckets of lake water. They had been visiting while we were with you!"

"Nature is alive and well," Carver commented.

After the visitors had walked out of sight, the camp became very quiet until finally the sound of a Super Cub engine starting filled the air. A couple of minutes went by before hearing the strong sound of the engine revving up. They all imagined Corky moving the throttle forward while the rudder pedals were pushed back and forth to keep the plane aligned with the snow tracks.

The engine roar quickly faded away to a very faint hum, and then, as Corky turned and returned towards the prospectors, the sound started getting louder.

Suddenly, N81C appeared overhead to one side of the three and as it turned back towards the lake. Paula was waving so they waved back.

"Wow! They flew from the cabin lake to here and back to there in less time than what it took us to just walk that same distance. I think I'm tired," Bobby announced.

Chapter 3 The Red Fox

"After we eat some more, let's set our packs along the side of our sleeping area," Marian stated before adding. "My pack has the food in it so let's set it by the Devils Club. Maybe that'll help keep the bigger animals and birds from grabbing what they might want, or think they want."

Carver nodded his head in agreement. "Good idea. And it'll keep a bear from tickling my toes."

"Just to be sure, maybe we should wrap your socks with Devils Club branches," Bobby teased.

"And may a cute bear cub tickle your ear and sit on your chest to keep you warm!" Carver said back as he carried the food to the Devil's Club and carefully set it under the long spiny branches.

"Boys! My goodness! You two sound like little kids," Marian said before she started snickering. "I must admit though that the thought of Bobby waking up with a bear cub on his chest gives me the giggles. And let's hope the Momma bear laughs and leaves quickly!"

As the three prospectors chatted about what they had done so far the sun went below the horizon and a gray dusk fell over the landscape. The conversation started to wind down and before long Bobby and Marian saw Carver was asleep.

"Carver's sure a good worker and companion," Marian said softly to her husband.

"Yes he is, and he handles a shovel like it's just a part of his arm. Tomorrow will be a workout for all of us, so we should get laid down too," Bobby replied.

"I'll put some more wood on the fire now and keep some close enough I can just reach it during the night."

"After a kiss good-night I'm going to snuggle into my sleeping bag Mr. Randall."

A Red Fox that was crouched in a Willow thick about a hundred yards away watched Bobby and Marian give each other a quick kiss and a hug.

The fire had died down and the people were now still and very quiet before the furry creature finally, and slowly, stood up and stretched. As the Fox scanned the siwash camp it suddenly smelled something different: a very light odor of meat.

The sly hunter crouched down and with its tail lowered, it slowly moved through the dim light cast by the fire. Soon it was at a spot on the back of the siwash. The smell of the meat seemed to be from a spot along the creek bank.

Carefully, the curious animal worked its way back and forth from Willow stand to Willow stand until it was about twenty feet from the Devil's Club.

The human food was very tempting until the hunter smelled and heard the motion of a different preferred food: a Red-Backed vole!

Even though a meal might be stolen from the pack, the fox didn't even try to get close to it. A memory of the Devil's Club spines causing a lot of pain flashed through its memory. So with a flick of its tail it ran after the Vole!

However, the furry little rodent barely escaped by scurrying below the Devil's Club branches and hid right under the food pack.

The Fox skidded to a stop just before it would have hit the spines. The predator stood still and stared at the possible meal and potential danger and wasn't sure what to do next when suddenly there was a loud pop from the fire pit. Quickly, the animal ran off to a Willow stand and disappeared.

After Bobby had tossed a small piece of wood onto the fire he recognized that there had been a movement close to the food pack. He leaned on one hand and used the other to block the firelight. Slowly his eyes adjusted to the darkness, but the animal that had been there was now gone.

Carefully, Bobby scanned the rest of the area, and then, as he looked up to check the sky for any weather clouds, he spotted the Northern Lights.

The bushes and hills behind him blocked a good look at the greenish wavy curtain of radiance, but what he did see brought a smile to his face.

Soon Bobby felt the heat coming directly from the fire as it burned the new wood and the warmth reflected off the tarp. The sensation made him drowsy again and after seeing that his companions were okay, he nestled back into his sleeping bag and quickly fell asleep.

Chapter 4   Sweet Cinnamon Rolls

"The green wavy motions of the Northern Lights are sure pretty," Mark whispered to his lady.

Corky didn't move as she enjoyed their embrace and replied, "I like the way it ripples from one side to the other just like a window curtain does when you shake it!"

"That's a good description, Miss Corcoran. I wonder if the Gold Diggers are watching it."

"Probably, but they were pretty tired when Paula and I left them. Dollars to donuts they're sound asleep."

"And speaking of sleeping, while Brenda and I were unloading my plane, we spotted a small dark animal that was moving slowly on the far side of the lake. Since we were about three-fourths of a mile away we figured it was either a large black bear or a small brownie that had just woken up from hibernating. We're sure it must have just come out of hibernation since no one has seen any bear sign until today.

"This bear finally stopped close to the south side of the trees and began digging where the snow had melted away. After kicking up a lot of dark dirt it would stop once in awhile and seemed to be eating something. Before too long it moved into the woods out of sight.

"It might have been looking for Skunk Cabbage. A spring bear typically eats that to clean out its system after hibernating, and that seemed to be a good spot for that early plant to be sprouting up. It produces a lot of heat as it starts growing and actually melts the snow that has been covering it. Besides locating the plant by its smell, the bear can see it and start their first meal.

"And speaking of eating, I'd like a hot cup of tea and a bite of Glenda's Cinnamon Rolls! Can I buy you one, Miss Corcoran?"

"Yes you may, Mr. Donnelly! I thank you very much for the hug and our time together. And it was a bonus to watch the Northern Lights. That will probably be the last time we can see them until next fall when the night's start getting darker, but I can sure take a hug anytime."

"And so can I!"

The two continued hugging for a few seconds more before turning away from the lake's edge to walk hand-in-hand back to the main log cabin.

As they walked through the doorway into the kitchen and dining area they were pleasantly surprised to see Glenda setting a pot of English Breakfast Tea and a plate of warm cinnamon rolls onto the table.

"My dear Glenda," Corky said excitedly as Mark helped take off her coat. "We're not taking you back to the rest of the world. Too many men would be trying to sweep you away and we would lose you. Thank you for having this all ready."

Glenda, while slowly shaking her head stated, "Not to worry! This is the world I love and to use one of Marian's phrases: 'It will take a real man to steal this Man-Hunter'."

"And besides," Paula chimed in, "I don't think I could let her go. She is a great help and just does her work so quickly, it amazes me."

"All of you amaze me!" Mark stated as he pulled a chair out for his lady to sit in.

"I ditto that," Corky commented as she slid a big hot Cinnamon Roll onto a small plate. "And I'll get fat if I keep eating all of this good food."

Mark and Paula tried to block the other from getting one of the rolls as Glenda finished pouring hot tea into the fourth cup.

"Because you're such a great cook, I'll secede and let you have the smaller piece," Mark teased.

With a grin Paula took the larger piece and put her hand over it to keep Mark from trying to grab it!

"You win this time, Miss Paula, the very awesome Great Cinnamon Roll Baker, but I don't recommend you look the other way!"

After pulling off a big soft chunk of a cinnamon flavored roll with her fork, Corky watched the white frosting drip onto her plate as she anxiously waited for the other three to get seated. As soon as they all sat down the roll quickly disappeared into her mouth. She closed both eyes and slowly rolled her head from side to side while making several loud humming sounds.

The three others dug in and soon all four were rolling their heads and humming.

Chapter 5   The Skunk Cabbage

Corky was just starting on her second bite as Paula finished and commented to Mark," Glenda said you two saw a bear at the lake's far side maybe digging for some Skunk Cabbage. I've known about bears that will dig into a shallow area of snow where that plant starts to sprout up. I've been told that the reason the plant pops up so early is it produces a lot of heat in that first shoot and the temperature is high enough to melt the snow.
"I was downwind from sprouting Skunk Cabbage one time and my goodness what a stink! I don't know what a skunk smells like, but this smelled like rotten garbage. No wonder flies and bugs go right to it."
"Many folks think Alaska's bears just eat meat," Mark stated, "which is what a Polar bear eats, but these black and brown bears are omnivores which means they eat meat and vegetation."
"Oh," Brenda suddenly exclaimed as she reached over to a slip of paper that was at the end of the table. "I'm glad you said 'vegetation'. Here is a list of the seeds Marian wants Tina to order from the seed catalog. Tina has a copy of the same booklet.
"I went through the mail you brought yesterday and so far there isn't anything to send back. The miners will probably read every catalog when they get back."
After Corky put the note into her shirt pocket Paula continued the conversation about garbage. "To keep our garbage from becoming a smelly issue we utilize almost everything here that is edible, but still it's difficult not to have some garbage.

"So that we don't have a bear problem, or at least for us to keep it minimized, we put the food garbage into a sealed can so it composts down. We're hoping we can get a garden going this year with it. The bears, hares, moose, voles, magpies, robins, and the many rodents will have to be kept out, but it's doable," Paula continued.

"I'm sure the bears will be here occasionally. They are curious animals and with the many different smells coming out of this camp, no doubt we'll get some visitors.

"The metal cans are washed and their paper labels taken off. The cans have a shiny slick side to them so I hang some in the garden to scare off birds. Plus they make a great wind chime by having four or five cans hanging in a row. You can get a soft almost musical sound from them when a breeze is blowing.

"At least three of those chimes will also be hanging in the garden to keep the birds away, and maybe the bigger animals like the bears.

"And to keep the squirrels, bears and porcupine out of the caches we wrap the poles with metal sheets cut from the big cans. You know the ones I'm talking about. They had pineapple or green beans or such in them. You take the bottom out just like you did the top, and then cut down the side and flatten out the metal. Nail one of them around each pole and they can't climb up it. So Presto! You now have a critter-stopper! Or you can use the metal five gallon cans the Blazo lantern fuel comes in.

"We'll need some fine mesh metal screen to keep the rodents and hares out.

"For the few garbage items we can't burn, like glass or plastic bottles, you've been flying them out to dispose of in the Homer dump."

While Corky and Brenda were eating, Mark stopped munching long enough to ask Paula, "Have you had any bear encounters in the many places you've been to in Alaska?" While she replied he continued eating the sweet cinnamon bun.

"Oh yes! Many times, but never anything serious. In Seldovia we might see black bears scurrying from house to house looking for garbage, or on the beach looking for fish scraps from the salmon canneries. The gurry, or fish waste, like the backbones, heads, and guts slid down a trough onto the gurry scow that was tied up next to the cannery dock, but sometimes pieces would wind up on the beach. A fish head or backbone would even get dropped by all the seagulls and eagles that were fighting with each other over the scraps. Once in awhile a bear would find those pieces, and then stick around waiting for some more.

"We didn't worry about having a bad encounter with any of the bears. Most bears don't want anything to do with people. If they're protecting their cubs or you invade their life space, then watch out. But an attacking animal is rare as they prefer staying away from humans and can be fun to watch, from a distance, of course!

"When those gurry scows got full, or at the end of a canning run, they were towed out and dumped way out into Cook Inlet somewhere on the outgoing tide.

"One cannery used a large revolving drum to heat up and dry salmon waste and then grind that into fish meal. The meal was bagged and used as a fertilizer in gardens and plant nurseries.

"Boy, what a stink came out of that place! Whenever you walked down the wooden boardwalk anywhere near that retort, you held your nose tight and kept your mouth closed! Whewee! What a stink!

"Well, anyway there wasn't much of a bear problem in town even with that yucky odor. But at the local dump you had to keep an eye out for bears. They'd be in the garbage piles looking for something to eat. Unless they had cubs or you got too close they ignored you."

"Neat story, Paula. Mom and Dad were floating the Yukon River on a research project when they stopped at Rampart," Corky stated as Paula sipped her tea. "They had heard stories of giant black bears rummaging in the Rampart garbage dump and yet other people said the bears were just the usual size ones. "So my parents decided to inspect the place to get an idea of what sized bears might actually be there.

"The two adventurers went to the dump that was over a mile from the village. On the dirt road to the site they saw lots of normal sized black bear tracks, but no bears. Carefully and slowly they approached the huge dump to keep from scaring any animals away, but it didn't matter as there wasn't a bear in sight! All the bear tracks and scat were of the typically sized bears, but not from any giants.

"Even the ravens were of the regular size, so after a couple of hours they went back to the village.

"Mom and Dad were visiting with the locals when a flat-bottomed river boat, called a Jon-boat, came from downriver with two men in it. They pulled ashore below the General Store and tied the boat to a beach log. One of the men in the boat said they had piled a bunch of fish bones and guts on the far side of the river in the usual spot away from the village. "And after having pulled away from the shore they waited to see if their favorite big black male bear, 'Yogi', would show up. Yep, it did! Immediately, the Giant dug into the fish pile.

"So my parents jumped into their boat and headed downriver. Before they even got to the dump site just below the first downriver bend they spotted Yogi and knew it was an unusually large size black bear.

"They didn't want the noise of the outboard motor to disturb Yogi so it was shut off. As they slowly drifted with the current, Yogi stood up. Mom said the bear had to be the largest black bear she had ever seen and viewed from the boat, the bear stood at least seven feet high!"

"That's a big black bear," Glenda loudly exclaimed.

"Dad tried to take pictures, but they had floated past Yogi before he had the camera ready. After moving out of sight of the bear the motor was started and back up the river they went, but the big animal was gone."

Corky stood up and finished with, "And so has this day! We've all had a long one and Mark and I need to fly out of here shortly after daybreak."

"That we do, Miss Corky," Mark responded while gathering up the dishes. "Bobby will be surprised that we brought over a chainsaw for you folks to use. And I want to do a quick review on the use of that chainsaw Brenda. I strongly suggest you wait until Bobby is here before you operate it.

"I'm confident you'll do a good job. However, if it doesn't start up like it should, or run smoothly, he'll know how to fine tune it.

"Also, the files for sharpening the chainsaw's cutters could use a wooden handle to keep from getting a blister in the middle of your hand.

"Your friend, Richard Williamson, in Homer uses one of these and likes it big time. They are heavy and noisy and the chain needs frequent adjustment to keep it tight enough, but it sure reduces the time needed to cut trees and logs for firewood. Someday I'm sure those saws will be built smaller and lighter.

"Don't forget to sharpen the cutters and at the same time keep the depth gauge filed down just enough that the sawdust looks like short confetti.

"It's better to use lots of that engine oil we brought to lubricate the chain so it doesn't get too hot.

"Since it is a two-cycle engine it uses a mix of two-cycle oil to regular gas. I wrote the oil-to-gas ratio on the side of the oil can since we talked earlier.

"I don't mean to sound like I am lecturing. I'm just concerned for your safety."

"No problem, Mark. I took it as a refresher on how to use that new gadget. We've plenty of firewood for several days so I'd probably wait for him to come back anyway. He can operate any machine he can get his hands on.

"The lanterns used the Blazo and you brought us two five gallon cans of that fuel this morning.

"And Carver is doing pretty good at figuring out how something works and what can be done to improve it.

"He fixed the broken center pole of his tent by cutting the bottom of the top pole even. Then he did the same to the top of the bottom pole. Using a hand drill he drilled a hole in the bottom of the top piece that would fit a 16d nail. Then he drilled the same size hole in the top of the bottom piece. After cutting off the head of a 16d nail he inserted it into both poles and tamped them together. The pole is real strong and works like a charm.

"We can now easily carry two full pails of water from the lake instead of one because Carver hand-carved a shoulder yoke that fits Mom or me.

"One of the buckets was leaking at the bottom so he pushed a nail through the tiny hole and made it bigger. After whittling a small piece of dry wood he stuck it in the enlarged hole and before long the wood swelled and the water stopped leaking. It hasn't leaked since.

"Also the antennae wire for that short-wave radio we use to stay in touch with Tina had dropped off the tree onto the ground. Without asking him to take care of it he attached a rope to the fallen end and climbed the tree and tied it off. It's stayed put real fine."

Paula, who had finished washing the dessert dishes while Glenda was talking then added, "That young man is a hard worker and never complains. He's also an avid reader. If he gets stuck on a word he asks one of us what it means. Sometimes we don't even know the answer so we all need a dictionary. When you folks come over the next time will you bring us a dictionary, and what's it called..? A Thesaurus! We'll surprise him with that."

"What a great idea Paula!" Corky exclaimed. "You folks have this cabin and the outside area looking just like a home and Carver seems to feel that. Mark and I are very pleased with what all you have accomplished here.

"And now it's time for me to get some sleep in the next room. Thank you, Brenda for the use of your bed. It has been a great day! Good night folks!"

After giving Mark a quick kiss good night, Corky went into the bedroom and closed the door.

As Mark opened the front door and before stepping out onto the porch he called back to the two ladies, "See ya'll in the morning!"

After closing the door he let his eyes adjust to the night before slowly moving over to the steps where the green wavy curtains of Northern Lights were still lighting up the night. Then, with a wary eye he checked to be sure a bear wasn't between him and the tent.

Chapter 6 Seldovia

When Mark heard, "Wake up Mister Lazy Bones! It's breakfast time!" he realized he had slept soundly despite his concerns about bears prowling around at night.

"The sun will be up before long", the voice continued. "And the ladies are ready to cook our favorite breakfast: Sourdough pancakes with homemade Rhubarb syrup and get this, real butter from a yellow can. Plus hot tea for me and just for you today, fresh brewed coffee!"

"Good Morning, Miss Corky! I'll be there in a flash to partake of the superb breakfast menu," Mark called back as he rolled out of the cot and started getting dressed.

"I think your idea of this beautiful place becoming a lodge for visitors has tremendous potential. The people will love all of the wildlife and scenery that's around here. Plus they can have the opportunity to pan and find gold in a real mining area", Mark excitedly pronounced.

In a few moments he had pulled back the tent flap and stepped out into the dawn's light in front of Corky.

"There is my Man! Not only is he a hard and smart worker, but he's very handsome. I'm a very lucky lady!"

After a quick kiss the two embraced for a long time until they heard a young female voice loudly calling out, "Come and get it before it gets cold. We'll eat it all if you don't get in here and get it!"

Corky was giggling as she responded to Brenda's make-believe temper tantrum. "Geez, Mark. I wonder what 'it' is! Brenda sounds real serious so we better go. I did hear your thoughts about this becoming a resort, so after we look over the other mining and cabin sites, let's talk about the idea in more detail."

"Sounds like a plan, Miss Corky. Shall we go and partake of the culinary delights created by the damsels?"

While holding hands the couple almost skipped over to the cabin's front door. Mark turned the knob and gave the heavy wooden door a solid push to get it open.

It had moved inward just a couple of inches before they were suddenly swept over with the mouth-watering sweet smells of hot sourdough pancakes and hot hickory-smoked bacon.

"Omigosh!" Corky exclaimed. "I didn't smell any of this wonderfulness a few minutes ago when I left to get Mister Sleepy Head. You ladies sure put it together quick. Just amazing!"

As Paula flipped two pancakes off the long black hot iron griddle onto a platter, Brenda was pouring coffee into Mark's cup. She tossed her head lightly from side to side and announced cheerfully, "Corky my dear, your English Breakfast tea is piping hot right from the pot. Mark sir, as you see your cup of java is as hot as lava. The warm sweet Rhubarb syrup was made last Fall'a for ya'lla by Miss Paula. If ya' wanna more Rhubarb syrup bring a big batch of Homer Rhubarb! Oh! And don't forget! Leave the leaves! They poison-us."

Laughter and light hand clapping filled the room as the three enjoyed Brenda's play on words.

After stirring in sweetened condensed milk and just before taking a bite of Sourdough pancakes dripping with warm syrup and butter, Corky responded, "We can sure do that and hopefully before we start flying in and out of the Lake Louise area."

Paula was sitting down to eat as she asked, "Have you hired another pilot to help you with all the flying that's coming up?"

"Yes. Jerry Winsmore. The one and the same pilot we met in Anchorage at Spenard's Piggly Wiggly store. We referred him to Harry Pridgetti in Bethel and after he spent a lot of hours flying over there he wants to do more flying over this way. Jerry prefers flying in the mountain and maritime climates like we have in Homer, Seward, and all of Southeastern.

"He was to arrive in Homer yesterday and his fiancé, Sharone, Harry Pridgetti's sister-in-law, will be moving over later in the summer. Pridgetti gave high marks to Jerry's flying and people skills and is sorry to be losing a good pilot.

"We need to get back to Homer as both of our Cubs will be converted from wheel-skis to just big Tundra tires. And the 206's need to have most of the arctic gear taken out. Plus, we need to get Winsmore oriented to who our clients are, what they look like, how to fly over to and land in different places and situations like Seldovia, or the beach at Halibut Cove, or the English Bay runway with its steep mountain right at one end, and so forth.

"Donnie, our aircraft mechanic and his helper, Doug, are anxious to get the changeovers done and all of the little detail work completed.

Paula was shaking her head while Corky was talking, and then said, "Wow! I feel tired listening to your list of what needs to get done!

"There's a little bit of trash for you to take out that we won't burn or can't recycle. We'll carry it to the Cubs and help you with the covers.

"After you take off we'll take care of these dishes so don't be concerned about them. And we'll call Tina so she'll know you are on your way."

"Thanks Paula," Mark said. "And after we're off from here and before we fly over the diggers, Corky and I will be filing separate flight plans to Homer with a stop in Iliamna for fuel."

In a few minutes the four had their coats on and were carefully walking over the wet narrow trail while carrying their personal gear and the bag of garbage. A Snowshoe hare's tracks could be spotted in what little snow was still left in the stands of willows and alders.

Off to their left side amid some tall Spruce trees a nervous chittering squirrel was upset about something.

"Look here," Mark called out to the three women who were behind him. He was pointing down at the trail by his feet. "Real fresh black bear tracks for the next thirty feet. They just got made minutes ago as the mossy stuff is still springing up. Right up there the animal went off to the left through those Willows and into the woods. I'm sure that's what the squirrel is upset about.

"Keep talking and hopefully it will just keep moving along. Bears rarely bother people and this one seems to be real skittish."

"Maybe it's the one Mark and I saw on the other side of the lake yesterday," Brenda loudly stated. "Those tracks are coming out of the Alders that are between us and the lake.

"Mom, do you have your pistol with you?"

"Yep! However, I don't think this bear wants to get up and personal. Those prints show that the animal is definitely on the move to get away from us! And I don't see any tracks of a cub.

"As you know the mother bears give birth to their babies during the winter hibernation. Unless something happened to the cub I don't think this bear was a female, or maybe it's a female that hasn't had a cub. We just don't know."

The trail meandered for several more yards through small Spruce trees and more brush before it ended at the southern end of a long open area.

Nearby the two single-engine tail-dragger type of aircraft were parked next to each other facing the morning sun waiting to get airborne.

As Corky was pointing at the planes while still walking along she commented, "I see that the heat from the sunlight is already melting the frost off the windshield and the leading edges of the wings."

In two minutes the four had started to unwrap the planes. Paula and Mark were uncovering his Super Cub, November-niner-one-zulu, as Brenda and Corky did the same on Corky's November-eight-one-charlie.

In a short time each plane's covers had been shaken dry and were loaded behind the back seat. The trash bag and Mark's personal pack had been secured on the back seat of Niner-one-zulu as had Corky's pack been secured in One-charlie.

The prior landings and takeoff had pressed the grasses and hillocks down considerably so what was left was a straight track the length of the field.

Corky was pointing at the track as she stated to the two women, "What we need to do ladies is get both of the planes moved into a good alignment with the tracks from yesterday's landings and takeoff.

"The wheel-skis can get damaged during a turn or moving under power on any rough terrain. To maximize a smooth takeoff, it'll be important for us to follow the same tracks out that we had created yesterday."

With just a few words spoken the four pushed and pulled to get Corky's Super Cub lined up with the tracks.

In a few more minutes they had moved Mark's plane to be sitting behind Corky's, but off to one side. As soon as she would be safely off the ground he would power his plane to the same takeoff spot she had just left.

Before climbing into Eight-one-charlie Corky looked over the area and announced, "Well folks, this will be our last day to fly in or out of this particular spot. What snow is still on these knobs of plants is hardly enough for the skis to ride on. And it is definitely not in any condition for using just the wheels. In fact, I'm concerned that our tail wheels might dip down into a hole and get caught.

"We didn't fuel up at Iliamna on our flight from Homer to here thus our aircraft weight is low. With our having just a few light items on board we should be able to get the plane's tail up soon. Then with some down flaps and lots of power we can get the load off the skis real quick.

"The main reason for having these wide skis that cover as much area as they do is like wearing big boots or snowshoes; there is more surface area to cover and thus less weight per contact area. In real terms, it means the skis cover more snow or slick plant area to help us stay up and to have more of whatever exists to slide on. We keep the skis as low as we can get them so only a small amount of the wheel shows. The process works for snow, wet bogs, muddy beaches, or combinations of such 'stuff'.

"After today we'll land on the lake which should be clear of any ice in three or four more days. Of course, by your calls to Tina and her relays to us, Mark and I will know the lake's condition before we come over.

"Our flight plans will be filed right after taking off and before checking on the gold diggers, and then away we go to Iliamna for fuel and to talk with Tina."

The four workers hugged good-by and the two pilots climbed into their respective planes.

As Paula and Brenda moved to be out of harms way they could hear Corky and Mark loudly calling out "Clear".

Within a few seconds both engines were running and were warming up as the mother and daughter team stood close to each.

"Mom, we should've brought the camera. Look how the water drops on those old Willow leaves are sparkling in the sunlight. And what a good shot we could get of the planes with those far off mountains in the background."

"Good idea, my dear Brenda. Let's put the camera by the door so it'll be easier to grab on the way out.

"Now both planes have gone through their engine run-ups and it looks like Corky is ready to take off."

Chapter 7   Sixmile Lake Brownie

"This is going to be a bumpy ride until I can get that tail wheel up and as soon as the wings have enough lift to get the weight off the skis."

Corky flipped the radio channel to the plane-to-plane radio frequency and called Mark.

"Niner-one-zulu. You ready to rock and roll?"

"Niner-one-zulu back. Yep. When you are at a hundred feet rock your wings that you're clear and I'll start my bumpy ride. Copy?"

"Roger on that Niner-one-zulu."

"Niner-one back. I'll fly slightly behind and on your left side. Copy Eight-one-charlie?"

"Sounds good. When I'm up I'll give Iliamna a call to file our flight plans. Let's go! Eight-one-charlie clear."

"Niner-one-zulu clear."

"Here I go!"

As Corky pushed the throttle in to get more power from the engine the propeller started turning so rapidly her eyes didn't even see the blades. The powerful force of the air from the propeller started moving the plane forward while being pushed back against the horizontal stabilizer and the elevator. About a second later enough force was pushing on the tail feathers, that as Corky pulled back on the control stick to move the elevator down slightly, the rushing air pushed against the elevator and forced the entire assembly to move up. As it moved up, the tail wheel moved up enough to clear the ground.

With the airplane already starting to move forward and with the tail wheel clearing the ground she lowered the tail slightly to increase the wing's angle of attack. With the aircraft moving forward faster and faster, the air pushing up created more lift that started transferring the plane's weight to the wings.

Eight-one-charlie had enough continuous forward motion that Corky could keep the airplane lined up with her intended ground path by using the rudder pedals. Even though the plane was being jerked from side to side and up and down by the rough vegetation and hummocks the plane was accelerating. Within about a hundred and fifty feet the skis were skimming along on the wet plant tops and the aircraft was almost flying.

"You can do it!" Brenda muttered to herself.

When Eight-one-charlie lifted off, Paula uncrossed her fingers and said to no one in particular, "Thatta girl!"

In a few seconds Corky waggled her wings to let Mark know she was at a hundred feet above the ground.

Immediately, the bystanders heard the blue and white November-niner-one-zulu's engine roar to life. In a few seconds the small aircraft was moving forward with its tail wheel above the ground. Mark got lined up with Corky's ski tracks and quickly traveled about the same distance to get airborne. At a hundred feet above the ground he rocked the wings to say "See ya' later" to the two women left on the ground.

As the sound of the two engines quickly faded away, the sheer silence of the country took over.

In a few moments Paula commented, "When all of a sudden you are alone in this majestic country, a person can feel really small!"

"'Small' works for that feeling of remoteness and so does 'insignificant'!" Brenda remarked.

Her mother nodded in agreement and added, "And even the word 'isolated' could be used, or 'tiny'.

"I wonder if Bobby, Marian and Carver feel less isolated when they hear the plane's coming?"

"That's a good question, Mom."

As the two caretakers turned to go back up the trail, the squirrel gave a quiet squeak somewhere in the trees.

Carver was on the gravel bar with his shovel when he paused a moment before announcing, "I hear airplanes coming this way."

"I hear them too," Bobby responded as he stepped off the creek bank and stood next to Carver. "And there they are. Two Super Cubs coming from the cabin area. I'll betcha that's Corky and Mark.

"Marian! It looks like we've got company!"

"Yep! I see them and they're starting a long climbing circle so they're not going to land here. Just wave a little bit, but keep doing what you're doing so they won't think there's any trouble down here. They'll see we're getting ready to start digging."

The three miners gave a quick wave and proceeded to setting up the shaker at the head of the gravel bar.

Both planes rocked their wings in acknowledgement before changing course for the 50 mile flight to Iliamna.

"Well, Mark, it looks like the miners are up and getting ready to do some more prospecting."

"Yep. They're quite a crew. One of these days let's join them and maybe we'll find some gold nuggets."

"I'm all for that, Mister Donnelly. Okay, its time to call Iliamna. Eight-one-charlie clear."

With a quick switch to the Iliamna Radio frequency, Corky called in and received the current weather and landing advisories.

In a few minutes the two had landed and after putting their flight plans to Homer on hold they were parked at John Barrie's FBO to top off their fuel tanks. Even though the Iliamna fuel was more expensive than Homer's, both pilots wanted full tanks to prevent an emergency landing from not having enough fuel.

Corky and Mark were by Mark's plane as they waited for a ramp person to come out. After a few minutes Mark tipped his head towards the building and quietly spoke, "Here comes our John, the Grump! I wonder if he's still looking for someone to replace Carver."

"Good morning, John!" Corky called out.

With a sour look on his unshaven face John lugged the fuel ladder to Corky's plane and was setting it in front of the port wing before he grunted, "Nothing good about it. I hired Pam from Nondalton to do this work. You'd think she'd be here by now. Can't get good help anymore!"

While going back to get the fuel hose a dusty green 1/2 ton pickup truck pulled up and stopped next to the FBO shed. A stocky girl stepped out of the truck with an air of confidence. She looked to be a teenager and wore faded blue jeans and a pair of worn leather boots A dark tan baseball cap covered her short black hair and she had on a brown zippered jacket.

Chapter 8 Pam

Without a word being said, but with a big smile on her round face, she scurried over to John and took hold of the fuel hose. While taking off his gloves and before he thrust them over to her, John said something, and then he shuffled into the building.

The smiling girl effortlessly dragged the hose over to Corky's plane. Before climbing up the ladder she stated with a chuckle, "Good morning! I'm Pamela. Good thing I showed up early. John might have had to do some work that he's not real fond of doing. Now we can't have that happen can we? All he said was, 'You're early'!"

In a few moments Pam had placed a rag around the fuel tank opening before taking off the cap and carefully setting the hose nozzle into the filler hole. Very slowly, she pulled the gas lever so there wouldn't be any splash back from the fuel rushing into the tank. As the aviation gas started flowing and without moving her eyes from her work, she spoke loudly.

"You must be Corky Corcoran and the good looking man is Mark Donnelly. I remember you both at Nondalton many times."

"Yep, I'm Corky and this is Mark. You look very much like our friend Alisha in Nondalton."

Pam quickly moved to short-talk as she explained her family connections. "She's Auntie. My mom, Marta is her sister. My dad, Samuelson, is brother to Charlie, Alisha's husband. Sisters married brothers.

"Sorry about Nels. He be friend to all; is missed by all. Miss him lots.

"Oh, I almost forgot! Not really!" Pam giggled. "Auntie says you'll get more smoked Pike soon! When weather much warmer."

"Now that's real special news for us," Corky said as she and Mark gave each other a high-five hand slap.

"How was Alisha's Pike fishing this last winter?" Mark asked while holding onto the ladder.

"We all did good," Pam replied while pulling the fuel hose nozzle out and let a small amount of fuel drip off and into the tank. The fuel cap was set securely in place and the area wiped with a rag.

After carefully climbing down the ladder with the hose in one hand she grabbed the ladder with the other. In a few moments Pam was set to refuel the starboard tank.

As Pam climbed up the ladder she explained when and how the Pike were caught.

"Last winter all the family made holes with our hand augers in the lake ice in the deeper water spots. We know from many years where those spots are.

"Oh, it was cold. And the wind blew so hard sometimes. We used our small wooden shovels to keep the slush out. My Momma is all wrapped up to stay warm and kneels on a Caribou mat and puts a colored jig with hooks into the water. The line is attached to a flat stick. The stick is easy to carry and doesn't get cold.

"She jerks the jig up and down just a bit. When a fish takes hold of the hook, Momma jerks the fish out onto the ice. They freeze rock hard. We take them home and keep them cold. Sometimes those fish are long. Like from your knee to your toes and longer. They got funny noses just like a snowplow!

"We use Pike in soups. Fry them. Bake them. Smoke them. Lotsa tiny bones, but good tasting fish. Mmmm!

"The fish we catch later this summer be bigger and smoke up real nice! Makes your mouth water, doesn't it?"

Corky used the back of her hand to wipe her mouth before she replied, "Yes! Yes! What a great fish story!"

"Hurry up, summertime!" Mark exclaimed excitedly, "I'm getting hungry."

Pam was securing the gas cap as she added, "This summer we just jig from the skiff and use a gill net. Much better weather for sure! Sometimes windy, but warmer than winter for sure!

"Okay Corky, you're plane is full of go-juice. Shall we move it to Tina's?"

Corky looked to Mark while asking, "Why don't you and I push mine over and by the time we get back Pam will have yours re-fueled?"

"Sounds fine with me. Pam did you get that?"

"Yep, I'll write down what I put in your plane Corky, and then I'll move over to Mark's."

"Moving the plane will be good for both of us as we need the exercise. By the way, how long have you been working for John? I haven't seen you here before."

"I started yesterday morning with him. Known him a long time. He wasn't sure a girl could do the job, now he thinks I've been doing it forever. I started helping fuel the planes at the lake and airstrip in Nondalton before I knew how to climb a ladder. Dad would hold me up and Charlie helped with the hose.

"When I heard Carver was gone I thought, why not try to get it. I want to work and see more of the world. So

I asked Grumpy John. He just grunted and said to always be here on time. No problem!

"I run my skiff from Nondalton down Sixmile Lake to the landing and drive here. Nice trip! Beautiful! And you never know what will happen.

"Why just this morning a small grizzly bear was real nosey around my truck. I waited in my skiff and ran the outboard motor loud a few times. Yelled, 'Go bear!' many times. Finally it moved into the bushes. I waited some more. Soon I saw a bear move along the lake bank a few hundred feet away. I figured it was the same bear. I tied up the skiff and ran to the truck. Here I am! Just another great day in the Great Land!"

"That's the right attitude to have Pam! Your journey is very much like what the folks in many of Alaska's coastal towns experience. They travel back and forth in skiffs or power boats to get to work and back home.

"In the Kachemak Bay area folks commute between Homer and Halibut Cove, Sadie Cove, Seldovia and Port Graham, Jakolof Bay, and such.

"And way down in Southeastern Alaska they travel by boat back and forth from Ketchikan to Gravina Island on a regular basis.

"Folks on the rivers like the Kuskokwim, Tanana and Yukon move around with boats.

"Having a bear encounter is just a part of living where the bears do. I don't know that any person would willingly give up their style of living because of the bears.

"Well Mark, we better get my plane pushed over as this lady is a real go-getter and she'll be done with yours in no time," Corky added as she was pushing on the tail to get Eight-one-charlie turned around.

In a few minutes the plane was parked in front of Tina's and after the brake was locked the duo headed back to retrieve Mark's. As they got closer they saw Pam putting the ladder back into its spot next to the FBO.

"Mark, why don't we go inside and sign for the fuel and maybe talk with John for a few minutes?"

"Good idea, Miss Corky. He might have some info on what's going on around here this summer and just maybe he might ask about Carver."

Pam led the way into the FBO's small office building and went around the counter to get the fuel paperwork ready to be signed.

John's loud and gruff voice filled the room as he talked on the telephone.

"Ain't no bear gonna bother ya if ya don't invite them in, Charlene. Quit putting your stinky garbage can on the porch. Ain't difficult to do. I gotta go. I got customers."

Before he had finished the last word, John had slammed the heavy black phone handle onto the cradle. "I can't believe how some people just ask for bear trouble. She's got a Momma black bear and cub that gets into the garbage can. Same thing last year!

"And when she gets fish, what's she do? The stinking fish carcass and guts are left lying on top of her garden. She thinks it'll fertilize the plants. I told her to chop the stuff up and mix it in with the dirt. No way! 'Too much work'; she says.

"Until Charlene changes her ways, the bears ain't gonna change theirs. No doubt this Momma bear is the same one that ate there last year.

"I see ya didn't bring Carver back with ya! He doing okay over there?"

"That's the very first time I've ever heard this man show any type of concern about Carver."

"He's doing real good John," Corky replied. "We're glad to have him working with us."

"That's good to hear. He's a good lad. And smart too. Keep him busy. You folks'll teach him more than I could.

"Nels and him got along real fine.

"I do appreciate how you folks keep your tab paid up. I thought with Marian gone Tina would be having a tough time. She's doing good.

"Some bear hunters were looking for a good pilot to fly them into bear country. Crazy people! I said you and Mark know the country. They'll be calling soon.

"How's Marian and Bobby now their married? They ain't been together long."

"This guy has told more and asked more than I've ever heard from him in any setting. Hopefully, he and Mark will keep talking while I get the paperwork finished with Pam."

When Mark felt Corky's gentle nudge against his back he started telling John, without saying a word of the gold prospecting, on how the cabin was spruced up, and the tents were set up.

When Mark described how helpful and willing Carver was, John just smiled, but he didn't make any comment about it.

Corky stepped up to the counter as Pam slid the fuel paperwork across to be signed. In a very quiet voice, the native lady stated, "That's the most I've ever heard John talk about anything, and he's being nice about it too."

"Well, Pam, it seems John just might be beginning to understand and accept that everything can't go the way he wants it to. Sometimes it takes a hard lesson for us to learn that. With Carver gone part of John is gone."

After the phone rang, and as John grunted a hello into it, Corky and Mark waved good-bye to him and Pam.

In a few minutes Eight-one-charlie had been moved to Tina's and after securing the brakes they walked into the house.

Chapter 9 The Decision

Tina said hello and started bringing the couple up to date. "Brenda radioed that you'd be here about now. I also heard when you closed the flight plans and watched you move the planes. I would have helped you, but the phone has been ringing off the hook. Lots of info for you when you're ready to hear it.

"There's hot water for tea, but I think after you hear the news you'll want to get to Homer soon."

"Is everybody okay?" Corky asked with a very worried voice.

"Oh! Everybody is fine. Sorry, I didn't mean to make it sound like some big emergency is going on over there. I've just had a lot of calls for flights that will keep you folks busy for awhile!"

Mark was taking his jacket off as he asked, "Whatcha got Tina?"

"First thing is that Jerry Winsmore called. He was at Mark's cabin with his gear, but he should be at the Homer Airport by now to meet with Donnie and Doug.

"Let's sit at the table where I have my notes.

"Dick Fritchman, the leader of that Oregon research team wants you to be picking up their gear and personnel at Lake Hood in Anchorage a week from today. The Lake Louise camp is to be set up by two weeks from today. The project has been changed. Instead of Caribou watching they will be studying 'the emerging of the bears' as he put it. I told him you'd be calling him tomorrow.

"The Coleman couple that was at Tutna Lake last year wants to be flown along the Skilak Lake area real soon. They want brown bear pictures.

The three friends sat down at the table as Tina went on with her list. "Don Volts has some freight to fly over here after you get his three man crew from Seldovia. Plus he has a bear story to tell you.

"Donnie said Corky's 206 is now at Beluga Lake with the repaired floats. It has a new three-bladed prop and the annual inspection has been completed. He asked if Corky's One-charlie Cub is going to be put on floats right away and parked next to your 206 Four-x-ray.

"It's taking me awhile, but I'm learning all of the tail numbers for your airplanes.

"The annual inspection for Mark's 206 Four-yankee has been completed.

"Cora said a Brown bear visited Anchor Point".

"My goodness! You've been busy," Corky responded. "Thanks for doing a good job keeping track of all this. I'm sure there will be even more activities as people recover from the quake.

"Now we need to sort out what to do first, and by whom, and when."

The shortwave radio by the window crackled before a woman's voice called out, "Tina you on? This is Paula."

Mark reached over to the set and grabbed the small handheld microphone. Before he answered Paula, Mark looked at Tina who just nodded for him to take the call.

"Paula it's Mark. How are you doing? Over."

"Hi. Did Corky get Marian's seed list? Over."

"Mark back. Yes she did. In fact, she handing it to Tina as we speak. Do you have anything to add to that list or your grocery list? Over."

"Paula back. No. Now we have a small black bear on our porch! We're not worried about it and when I get off

I'm going to scare it with a shot from my pistol. The valley people okay? Over."

"Roger on the black bear and the valley trio. We're just about ready to leave for Homer. Tina's waving hello to you. Over."

"Paula back. Here's a wave from us to you all. Have a safe trip. I'll leave the radio on for another half hour. It'll be on for this afternoon's schedule. Over. Out."

"Copied. Mark out."

After hanging the microphone back on its hook and turning to the table Mark stated, "There's sure been a lot of bear activity. I wonder if the quake and its aftershocks have aroused the bears early. Although, this is about the time they would be out of hibernation."

"Hard to know," Tina replied. "Some springs lots of bears. Some years just a few. Just maybe they're looking for you to chew on," she teased.

"I don't have enough fat on me to satisfy any bears!"

Tina and Mark quickly turned and both of them stared at Corky.

"Don't look at me and make comments about being bear bait!" Corky laughed while putting both of her hands up with the palms towards the two smiling friends.

"Okay, moving on! Instead of waiting until we get to Homer to find out what Fritchman wants, I'll call him now to get more details of what his plans are. Maybe we won't be involved. Maybe we will."

Corky moved over to the telephone while Mark stood up and stated, "You make the call and I'll make the tea!"

Tina started reading over Marian's seed list as Corky direct-dialed Dick Fritchman.

In a few minutes the three were drinking a cup of hot English Breakfast tea as they kept busy.

Mark and Tina were reviewing the fuel and business bills while Corky kept on talking to Dick.

The short wave radio under the ramp window emitted a crackling sound for the umpteenth time when at last Corky put the phone down. After a sip of her tea she set the empty cup down and simply said, "Whew!"

As if to keep her friends in suspense she took her time to slowly refill her tea cup; put in Sweet Condensed Milk, and then slowly stirred it before she started talking.

"Okay, here's what I've got and I do think it's a real mess. I talked with Gary who said Fritchman wouldn't be back for thirty minutes or so, but that Gary could answer a lot of our questions.

"There will be Dick and a five-person crew. So there are a total of six people. They'll have the use of three Army tents. One big tent is for everybody to bunk in. A second big tent is for cooking, eating and a place to meet. A smaller tent is for supplies.

"He wants us to land on the dirt road with the tents, two people and as much of their gear as we can load in one of our plane's about two days from now. The two men will haul the tents and gear to the lake and load it into a skiff.

"They are renting the skiff and motor from a guy living at Trapper's Den. He'll be on his way to Lake Louise the day after tomorrow pulling a boat trailer and skiff with the outboard motor, gas, oars, and oil.

"The two guys we deliver will take the skiff and gear to a spot that is about five miles north from of the passage between Lake Susitna and Louise.

"The other four people are to be flown to the lake camp the next day. They'll have their own gear and the research gear with them. Their intent is to be in that area for a month before getting back to Anchorage.

"Gary said that Dick wants us to use both of our Cubs to fly crewmembers over specific land areas. The idea is to map out vegetation that is in the area within a certain distance of their camp.

"That means both Super Cubs are to be on-site at the same time for the first week after the camp's set up.

"And we will stay at the camp for that week.

"For the following three weeks they will have two-man teams hiking out to do on-site general surveys of trees, bushes, animals, etc. in those flown over areas.

Mark interrupted with a comment, "That's pretty flat country. I wonder if any of them have ever been there before and comprehends how hard it is to walk through that muskeg, willows, tussocks, alders, hidden creeks, and such."

After a quick sip of tea, Corky went on, "Don't know the answer to that. Anyway, we'll fly in and pick them up from the same spot where we took them in originally."

The room was silent for a few moments. Suddenly Mark and Tina flooded the room with their questions.

"Those army tents are heavy and bulky. It sure will take more trips than he realizes to get all of his gear and people up there. Why not fly from Lake Hood right to their lake site instead of using the skiff from the road?"

"Do you two need your own tents? And who's feeding you? What food, etc. do you need to take with you?"

"We'll need to take in extra avgas as Gulkana is the closest spot to refuel. Is he paying for and supplying the extra fuel?"

"How and when will you be staying in touch with me here in Iliamna?"

"Can you have Jerry do the local work, and with what plane or planes?"

"What contingencies are there for any delays because of bad weather?"

"Will they have a shortwave and or CB radio?"

"Who's going to support the prospectors for supplies or whatever else they need?"

"I thought it was a caribou research study, so what happened to that project?"

Corky tried to jot down some points about what was being asked.

Finally Mark and Tina paused to catch their breath so Corky quickly said, "And now you know why I wanted to talk this over with you two.

"First thing is this is a portion of their caribou study as they want to better understand why there can be so many animals in certain areas and not others. My thinking is to ask the natives. They've been hunting there for centuries.

"They want the skiff to be available to get back and forth between the road system and the camp at any time. That's fine, except both of those big lakes can be hit with extremely strong winds. Many skiffs have been flipped as you have to almost go broadside to the wind for about twenty miles.

"Mark's 206 on wheels can land on the road and I can land on the lake that's at the road's end, or by their lake campsite. We can even convert his plane to floats if Dick will agree to changing parts of his plans.

"I think that Jerry Winsmore could handle our flying needs down this way. He'll have either a 206 or a Super Cub available.

"I'll give Dick another call with these questions. He's a few hours ahead of us time-wise so I need to get my thoughts in order and get him called."

Tina and Mark went back to their paperwork and the radio crackled some more.

Paula radioed in right on schedule to check for any updates. When Mark answered the call, he asked her what had happened with the bear. She said it ran away after the pistol shot, and then she asked why they were still in Iliamna. Mark replied that there were more questions needing answers about the "Louise" trip so the project leader was getting called again.

Finally, Corky hung up the phone and sipped the last drop of tea from her cup. Tina offered to make another pot, but Corky just shook her head.

"Okay. Everything makes more sense. I was able to talk with Dick instead of Gary. There have been some significant changes.

"First thing he said is the tents are not the heavy canvas Army tent. They are an Army wall style of tent made with much lighter material and they weigh about eighty pounds each. The smaller tent weighs about sixty pounds and each tent is in a big bag.

"One of the crew is a woman. She and I will share the supply tent while Mark and the others will be in one of the big tents.

"He agreed that we should fly most of the crew and the gear directly to the camp. The camp will be about fifteen, not five miles from the road.

"The extra outboard gas, the lantern fuel and most of the food supplies and other gear such as the surveyor tripod and such, will be trucked by two men to Lake Louise from Anchorage. The truck will be left there in case it is needed.

"So, four people will fly with us to the lake site with the tents and personal gear. We will fly back to Homer to get the Super Cubs on floats and return back there as soon as possible. They should have the camp completely set up within two days.

"None of the six people have been in Alaska before. Except for Dick, the others are graduate students working on habitat degrees. This place was selected by what a biologist who had hunted bear in the area a few years ago told Dick.

"This could easily become a nightmare adventure with these six Cheechakos, City Folks, Greenhorns, City Slickers, or whatever you want to call them.

"He agreed that there wouldn't be any loaded weapons in the airplanes. Once they are on site everyone will be wearing a pistol in case of any bear problems. Also there will be a rifle with each group that will be doing the habitat studies away from the camp.

"And they are not there to study caribou. Other than learning about the types of plants and terrain in the area, they hopefully will see bears, moose and other animals.

"Corky," Mark asked, "are we sure we want to be involved in this project? Their conditions keep changing with each phone call. Who know what changes will occur without any prior notice given to us.

"These folks are unaware of and are certainly not prepared for the wilderness challenges they will have to contend with up there.

"Not just a few, but many of those challenges can be easily overwhelming for even many long-term Alaskans, native or otherwise.

"How about disturbing a bear before it is ready to come out of its hibernation? There are so many stories of injuries hurt by such unhappy critters.

"A small bear getting into their camp like what Paula is dealing with right now can become a real serious problem if their not careful on handling it. If anyone gets panicky the bear might charge.

"What about how they will handle the mass of mosquitoes that get into your eyes and ears. They can completely cover a head net to the point you can barely see where you're going. Many animals like caribou have gone crazy because of the shear numbers of bugs and their constant noise. Most repellents do very little, if anything, to even slow down their invasive presence.

"There are the biting bugs like the swarms of No-See-Ums and the White Sox. Mosquitoes will suck your blood while the White-sox and No-See-Ums leave a painful hole.

"What about the awful Black Flies that haven't any boundaries. They'll get in your face and ears and crawl into your clothes and a bite will be sore for days. They just won't go away!

"How will those newcomers deal with the incredible remoteness of the Interior? If a person isn't familiar with being away from an urban area and are thrust into it, the wild remote life can be completely unbearable."

Tina and Corky were listening intently to Mark, and when he paused for a moment, Tina added to the list of concerns. "I strongly agree with Mark.

"When that commercial plane stops here some of those passengers get off to stretch their legs and feel out the country. They suddenly get hit on how big this country is and they can't wait to get to a town.

"I think those students shouldn't be thrown into such a wild place without being better prepared.

"What if they see a brown bear and cub and want to get close? They are lots of bears in that Lake Louise area. Most bears will leave a person alone, but those Momma bears aren't the least be afraid to angrily protect their cubs.

"Many of the Alaska newcomers get a real sense of fear, almost a panic, when they hear a pack of wolves howling. Or they see one up close.

"I had an incredibly wonderful experience with a lone wolf up there when I hunted for ptarmigan off the Lake Louise road. It was during a real cold winter and the silence was almost scary. It was so quiet there wasn't any sound except when your clothes brushed a bush or branch. And you could actually hear your heart beating in your neck!

"I was sneaking around a tall stand of frosted willows and was on the edge of a small clearing as I came face to face, maybe fifteen feet away, from a lanky black and tan wolf. We both stopped and looked straight into the other's eyes.

"I'd never felt such a positive connection with any animal before and it left a lasting impression on me. After about a minute we moved away from each other very quietly. I didn't fire my gun and I sure didn't say anything to the other hunters.

"Well anyway, back to the Concord group. Are those people prepared for such an event? It sure doesn't seem like they are."

With a small shuffle in her chair she continued, "Now for a business point of view. Do we need to be dealing with a poorly managed outfit that hasn't kept us informed in a timely manner of their many changes? And have any of them asked how the changes might affect our plans? And being sure we get paid for those changes, or even just getting paid concerns me."

"Those are all very good points for us to have concerns about," Corky stated as Mark nodded his head in agreement with Tina. "I'm going to call Mr. Fritchman and withdraw our involvement.

"There is so much business coming our way we don't need to take on such a confusing project like this.

"I'd sure like some more of that delicious tea," Corky stated as she went over to the telephone.

Mark and Tina finished their paperwork just as Corky finished the call to Dick Fritchman.

"I didn't give Mr. Fritchman all of our reasons for not getting involved at the present time, but he said he felt the cancellation was going to happen.

"The Trapper's Den fellow had just pulled his deal because the man didn't want his skiff and gear operated by inexperienced people.

"Dick said he was having second thoughts about the project anyway. The travel to Alaska was an iffy deal due to the earthquake damaging runways, delaying airplane flights, inconsistent mail delivery, questionable sources for fuel, food, and so on.

"He said he would be sure and recommend us to others because we've been so upfront with him.

"Frankly, I'm relieved."

The three poured another round of tea and touched each others cups to salute their decision.

Chapter 10   North Fork Visitor

"Now back to Tina's list," Corky directed.

"Jerry will be busy with Donnie and Doug so we can talk with him in Homer.

"Mark, would you mind calling Don Volts now and find out who the men are that need picking up in Seldovia and how soon?

"On second thought what do you think about Jerry using your 206 to get the Volts' Seldovia crew, and then bringing Volts' load and crew to Iliamna? Donnie has a set of keys for your plane.

"And Mark, if you agree, let's have Donnie put my Cub on floats and keep yours on your tundra tires, at least for awhile.

"Good idea on both accounts, Corky! I'll tell Jerry how we fly to the end of the Spit and across to the other side of the bay to be closer to land. I'll also let him know that some pilots take off from the Seldovia strip without any radio warning."

Corky added, "Good! Also have him keep an eye out for the black bears looking that are looking for salmon in the slough by the airstrip.

"Also please tell him about the bears that like to eat those blueberries and salmonberries that grow at the base of the hill south of the strip.

"Ask Don what's his bear story. There are a lot of black bears out the East End Road where so many of us live. Maybe a bear broke into his shed. They love to grab for something that's above them and in the process they typically crush whatever they are standing on.

"It seems to be that the bigger the mess they can make the happier they are.

"I'll call Cora when you're through and bring her up to date on what our plans are, or maybe I should say what we think they are going to be.

"There are lots of brown bears around Nikolaevsk every summer.

"In fact, there are lots of brown bears over most of the entire Kenai Peninsula. Some of the largest brown bears in the world occur over there.

"I remember a black and white picture of a six-foot tall man holding a rifle at arms length while standing next to a brown bear hide. The hide had been stretched and nailed onto the outside wall of a homesteader's barn up in Happy Valley. That bear appeared to be ten feet long from its nose to its hind end.

"That homesteading family ate the bear meat for a long time and used the bear fat for cooking. I ate some oatmeal cookies they made from that fat. They had a strong taste and would be real good to have now with this great tea you made Mark!

"I'll call the Coleman's and find out if they have a date in mind to be flown to Skilak. Do they want to camp for a few days, take sightseeing trips, or just what? You know some of Alaska's biggest brown bears live in that Lake Skilak area.

"My 206 is at Beluga Lake ready to fly so I can use it to take them where they want to go, where's there enough water of course.

"Well, I've talked enough for now, and I need to look over that paperwork."

Mark went to the telephone and was making his call to Jerry as Corky and Tina started going through the pile of business papers.

While talking with Tina Corky didn't realize she was constantly rubbing the bear cub pendant that was on her necklace. The animal figure had been carved by Nels from a small golden brown agate and was a caring gift from Mark.

"You have done a great job keeping all of this 'stuff' organized Tina. Let's go through it as Mark talks to Jerry and before my call to Cora and the Colemans plus we need to be leaving soon."

Several minutes passed before Mark finished his call and update the girls, "Jerry said he looks forward to the trip and will be taking my 206 to Seldovia. We discussed how the maps will not be as accurate for the many beaches that have been affected by the quake. The maps have never been real good on details anyway, but they can offer some good guidelines.

"He knows to keep track of his time and the engine time, the type of load, its weight, the passenger list, and so forth and so on.

"When he gets back to Homer he'll refuel and load up Volts' cargo that Don will be delivering to our tie-down spot. He'll be here within four hours.

"I was also able to talk with Donnie and gave him the okay on putting your Cub on floats and have my Cub wear the tundra tires."

"It sounds good, Mark. I'll give Cora a call."

The radio by the window crackled just before Corky dialed her sister in Nikolaevsk. Someone in Pile Bay was calling Igiugig, but when she realized it wasn't a serious call Corky started dialing in her sister's phone number.

"This dial-it-yourself system sure is quicker than the old system of having to talk to an operator first. I used to wait and wait for one of them to …"

The phone rang twice before a lady answered the call and Corky heard, "Hello! This is Cora!"

"Hi, Sis! It's Corky! How's life in Nikolaevsk? I hear you've got a bear story to tell me."

The two sisters talked about the Lake Louise project; Jerry's flying Volts' crew and cargo; how the prospectors were doing; and general chit chat until finally Cora told her bear story.

Corky was laughing as she commented, "Oh my! That could have turned out badly if they had gone after the bear. You bet I'll tell Mark and Tina.

"Mark and I will be flying out of here in thirty minutes, but I need to call the Colemans first.

"Hi to Tall Man! Love ya, Sis", Corky stated before she hung up the phone.

"Cora had quite a story. Let's see if I can get it right.

"As you know at Nikolaevsk the bears come through now and then in the spring and summer season. Mostly they're brown bears. There aren't any dogs in the village so when a bear does come around people phone each other about the visitor. Or they yell out an announcement to a neighbor who then yells out the message to another one and so forth.

"The other day her and Lydia Fefelov drove to Homer to run some errands, get groceries, and simply enjoy the sunny spring day.

"On the way back home they decided to drive to the Cook Inlet beach at the mouth of the Anchor River which is not very far from Nikolaevsk. It is a very beautiful place and the sun was shining.

"They took a long walk on the gravel and sandy beach and saw that Mt. Redoubt had steam spewing out near its top as did Mt. Iliamna. There were even wisps of steam at Augustine Volcano.

A few Bald Eagles and the usual seagulls and shorebirds were flying by, but nothing out of the ordinary. Cora said there was a big seal way out from the beach and Lydia had found a small pretty agate and a stone with a hole in it.

"When they got back to the car, Mack McCann came over to say hello and visited with them for awhile. Mack and his wife, Melanie had had quite an experience that morning. They live in a small cabin that overlooks the North Fork of the Anchor River, maybe a mile and a half from the beach.

"They were on their porch admiring the river that was about a hundred yards away and maybe fifty feet below the level of the cabin. They'd been talking about how tall the Willows and Alders had already grown this early in the year. Just as she pointed at a spot along the river's bank a Brown bear got up and stood on its hind legs!

"The bear didn't look up in their direction. It just stood tall and slowly peered around its general area before dropping back down. And then it just plain disappeared!

"The couple kept looking for the bear, but they never saw even a branch move!

"Cora said she shuddered from fright as if she had been there to see the big brown bear.

"Mack laughed as he said they didn't have any desire to walk down and find it to take pictures!"

The three were laughing about Cora's story when the telephone rang.

Chapter 11   Maclaren River

"Hi! This is Tina. How may I help you?"

"Hi, Jerry! Yep, I'm the goalkeeper over here. How are you doing?" she asked while giving Corky and Mark an impish grin.

The two kept busy talking as Corky and Mark waited anxiously. Tina finally told him to wait a minute while she asked Mark a question.

"Mark. Jerry wants to know if there is anything else he is to do besides bringing the Seldovia crew back to Homer and flying the hardware and crew to Iliamna."

"Nope. Just tell him he's to fly back to Homer when he's done here."

"Jerry! Mark says just fly back to Homer when you're done over here," Tina said with a big smile. "I'm looking forward to meeting you! See ya' later."

Tina turned and saw Corky and Mark watching and listening with smiles on their faces. Tina's face turned a bright red from blushing.

"Okay! Okay! I know he's got a fiancé, but if he's as good looking as he sounds, oh that would be something!"

"Ow! That sure didn't come out right!"

"Not to worry Tina," Corky said with a chuckle as she gave her friend a quick hug. "Maybe one of the guys that he's bringing over will become your lucky Man-friend!"

"And who knows Tina," Mark interjected. "He could be an electrician and just shock you!"

Both Corky and Tina pretended they were throwing a glass of water at Mark as he quickly ducked away.

The radio crackled as if it enjoyed the humor too.

"Okay. I need to call Mr. and Mrs. Coleman and find out what they want to do," Corky said as she went to the phone. With a few quick turns of the rotary dial she called the number Tina had written on a piece of paper.

"This is an Anchorage number. I wonder what they're doing in Anchorage so early in the year."

The Coleman's phone rang five times before an answering machine came on with a pleasant female voice asking the caller to please leave a number and Paul or Angela would give a call back as soon as possible.

Corky left her name and Tina's number and the date and time of the call, and then she put the heavy handle back into the cradle on the top of the black telephone.

"I tried and we do need to get to Homer."

"Well, Tina, I left them a message to call here. You know I think it's time to put your number on my answering machine, and Mark's, if he's agreeable to it. So now if we get a business call at our phones and we're not there to answer it, they can call you. They should be calling you anyway. We're getting too busy to be missing business calls. It will take a little bit of time, but eventually you'll be getting the majority of the calls."

"I'll do the same," Mark stated as he grabbed Corky's coat and helped her put it on.

"Okay folks. Good idea. That should help a lot. And we still don't know what Don Volts' bear story is about. Have a great trip back!

"Hey, wait just another minute if you will. I've got one more bear story. This is when we were hunting way north in the Maclaren River area east of Cantwell on the Denali Highway. The road is between Cantwell and Paxson.

Usually my family hunts around here, but we felt adventuresome. Want to hear it?"

Both of the pilots quickly replied to Tina's question. "Of course," Mark said while Corky remarked, "then we have to hightail it out of here!"

"We were hunting caribou and moose in the remote Maclaren River country about halfway between Cantwell and Paxson. The hunting party consisted of five adults that included my two parents, and two of us kids. Well the group was using a military surplus track vehicle called a Weasel that kept losing one of its tracks. That was a very common problem with them things. Now we're way back off the dirt road where there's absolutely nobody else to help fix it.

"My brother was about 12 and our friend Charlie was a grown man. The two were told to go hunt something to eat as there were too many helpers. So off they went with rifles and walked up and down them hills. Some of them were pretty flat on top. Those hill tops were covered with lichen and short bushes, but the draws were full of dwarf trees, tussocks, Willows, Alders, and wet muskeg. In the draws it was tough walking through that brush and such.

"They did scout the area for about a mile and half from where the Weasel had broken down. After stopping on top of a short ridge and not finding any animals or tracks, they figured it was time to get back to the others.

"On the way back they saw my mother standing on top of a bare knob waving at them. So they waved back and kept on going along, up and down the hills.

"When they'd get to the top of the hill they'd look over and she'd be waving at them again. They waved back and kept trekking along in a long arc back to the camp.

"Finally, when they were within talking distance she yelled out angrily, 'Didn't you see me waving at you?'

"Yes, they said and we waved back. Is everything okay back here?

"She just put her hands on her hips and barked back, 'Every time you two boneheads went off a hill and down into a draw, a big brown bear would come out of the one you just left and mosey to the top of the hill. He's been following you for a mile. He left you three hills ago.'"

"Charlie, a quiet sort of guy, asked her, 'Why didn't you shoot your rifle in the air to warn us?'

"I don't remember what she said, but frankly, I never did get scared about that bear. If it wanted them, it sure would've gotten them. Most bears don't want to deal with people so I think that one was just being curious. Maybe it figured out my mom would shoot it!"

The three were chuckling as they walked to the two parked planes.

In a few minutes the pilots had performed their walk-around pre-flight and were buckled in while Tina moved away to a spot by the house. When the pilots called out "Clear" she gave a thumbs-up to indicate she didn't see anyone near the planes.

After the engines had warmed up, the Super Cubs taxied out to the main runway with Eight-one-charlie in the lead and Mark about four plane lengths behind it. He kept himself situated off to Corky's left side to be sure she could see him at any time.

Tina smiled as she watched with amazement as the two aircraft powered up and as one unit moved faster and faster down the runway. After a few seconds both planes lifted off the runway at the same time. Before they were at the far end and high enough the Super Cub formation made a very smooth left hand turn towards Lake Iliamna and Homer.

Chapter 12 Skilak Lake Follower

The slow moving airplanes flew east along the upper edge of Lake Iliamna, and then past the Pedro Bay airstrip. They increased their altitude as they moved closer to the open Cook Inlet waters. When they arrived at the south end of the semi-active volcano of Mt. Iliamna, their altitude was high enough to cross the dangerous waters.

The long fifty mile crossing over the cold Cook Inlet to reach the Anchor Point didn't have a safe place to land an airplane that wasn't equipped with floats. Both pilots knew that the higher they were able to be, a longer glide path could be used to get them closer to a safe shore in case an engine quit or they had some other serious malfunction.

Rich Williamson was watching from the FBO as the two planes made a perfect formation touch-down at the Homer Airport. He knew both aircraft would need to be refueled so as he waited with the ladder and fuel hose the two Super Cubs taxied up to the FBO's ramp.

Corky was just climbing out of her Super Cub when Rich exclaimed, "Beautiful landing, Corky!"

"Thank you, Rich! Mark and I haven't flown formation much, but so far it's been smooth."

"In fact, all of the many things Mark and I do together have been going smoothly.

"Is ever going to ask me to marry him?"

Mark parked his plane to one side to keep the ramp from getting crowded. He was walking up to Corky when Rich loudly proclaimed, "That was a very impressive landing Mark. You two sure do fly together well."

"Thanks, Rich. Miss Corky always sets a great example on how to fly an airplane.

"How is your flying coming along?"

"I now have a commercial license for single-engine land. I'm going to work with Fish and Game this summer so I'll be leaving here pretty soon."

Corky and Mark quickly looked at each other before Corky asked, "Where in this great State will you be going to? We'll sure miss you."

"Thanks for the compliment. Well, so far I've been told I know I'll be involved with salmon egg research at the stream in Mallard Bay up towards the head of Kachemak Bay, and the same thing in a few streams on the Outside Beach area.

"Sometime in all this I'll be doing Herring catch sampling work in Seward. Then I'll be backpacking gunny sacks up the Russian River trail for the fish weir on the Upper Russian River area. So it will be a busy summer."

"Wow!" Mark said. "It sounds busy. Just be careful about the bears. The black bears are thick on the south side of Kachemak Bay and there are lots of brown and black bears up in the Russian and Kenai drainages."

Rich was nodding his head when he replied "I will definitely be careful. I've already had a variety of bear experiences in my short life.

"There was a fellow here yesterday that told quite a story about his close encounter with a bear up in the Cooper Landing area. When I'm finished getting this plane fueled up I'll tell you about it if you want me to."

"There's been a lot of bear experiences in this country and we definitely want to hear all that we can," Corky said. "Maybe more bears are out of their dens since we had the big quake and those aftershocks. I'm sure the bears got woke up early."

After Rich twisted the fuel tank cap on tight the fuel area was wiped with the rag even though not a drop had been spilled. When the ladder and the fuel hose were moved to the starboard wing with Corky's and Mark's help and the fuel was going into the tank, Rich proceeded to tell the bear story he had heard the day before.

"This young guy, who was about my age, was in the Runway Café telling this scary tale. I'll try to tell it just like he did so here goes.

"Willy and I was real tired after a long drive to the Skilak Lake boat launch from Anchorage. The last part of that Skilak dirt road was rough on us and on the boat and trailer. Once we finally did get there it didn't take us long to get that skiff into the water. We got our hunting gear loaded before we got the outboard motor started up and off we went.

"We didn't have in our plans to hunt that first night once we got across the lake and over to the southwest shore. You do know where I mean I am sure. Just past the spot the Kenai River flows out of Skilak Lake. We figured a moose would be over there since there wasn't any road. We'd hunt the next morning. We'd stay for two days, maybe three if need be and the weather held out good.

"We set up our siwash camp and fixed some dinner before we checked around our camp for a sign of any moose. We did find a few fresh tracks and droppings so we knew moose were close by.

"We were in a mixed forest area. Sometimes there would be a clearing here and there. We sure didn't want to walk into the open if we didn't have to. Better to walk along the tree line or along the huge Alder patches to avoid being seen.

"We figured out the next day's hunting strategy so we went back to camp. We ate some before we sacked out.

"We got up early and we were real quiet. The fire had gone out. We left it out. We didn't eat but a snack. We sure didn't want the moose to know we were going hunting for them.

"I went to the northeast towards the River and Willy went to the left, sorta to the west. We agreed we'd make big circles and meet back at the camp. If either of us shot the rifle the other was to come over and help out.

"After awhile, probably thirty minutes or less, I was going real slow and quiet-like past the Alders on my left. On my right were small Black Spruce trees. They can be eight feet tall and a hundred years old. Sometimes you can't walk through them when they've got their branches so tightly mixed in with the other tree's branches.

"Then all of a sudden the hairs on the back of my neck went up. There wasn't any sound from me or anything. Every squirrel had gone quiet and the Camp Robbers had just flown away without a bit of noise. That's real unusual.

"I stopped and real slowly looked behind me. I didn't see anything to be concerned over, but I did undo the safety on my rifle just in case I was going to shoot something real quick. I decided then to go around the big Alder patch to see if anything might have been following me. It took me a few minutes to get that walking done.

"When I got back around to my tracks I looked down and saw huge bear prints! They was placed right on my boot prints! That big Brown bear had to be just around the other side of the bushes from where I was standing!

"My boots are almost a foot long. The width of those bear tracks was slightly longer than my boot!

"I didn't panic. You don't ever want to panic. If that bear had really wanted me it would've done it already. If I ran the bear would probably run after me to get me.

"The best thing was to slowly go back to the camp on my old trail as I knew where it went. I frequently looked behind me on the way to check if the bear was there. It wasn't anywhere in sight.

"I found the spot where that big bruiser bear's tracks first came onto mine. It had started to track me from about half the way from our camp.

"Well, I made it back okay. I sure kept my ears and eyes wide open and my rifle ready. It was only about fifteen minutes later and here comes Willy!

"Okay I'm through with this plane Corky. Let's get it moved back and get yours over here Mark. I can finish the guy's bear story then."

In a few minutes the three had moved Corky's Cub One-charlie plane over to its tie down spot next to where her Cessna 206 would have been parked. Mark's Cessna 206 was gone and was supposedly on its way to Iliamna.

It didn't take long for the efficient trio to have Mark's Super Cub pushed up to the fuel ramp. In a few moments Rich had the ladder and fuel hose in place and was filling the port wing tank when he continued the story.

"When Willy got up to me I asked him if he was okay.

"He said he was. He said it was the first time he'd ever been snookered from behind by a bear.

"We figured the bear followed me out of plain curiousness before he picked up Willy's smell. The bears are real good at smelling weak odors.

"Anyway, the bear had also followed Willy for a ways too. When Willy felt his hair go up he made a big circle back and found the same size tracks I had found. That's when Willy decided he'd come back to camp.

"Later, after some lunch, we set out again to get a moose. I found one a ways from the camp in a different direction and bagged it. Willy came over and between us we got it cleaned up. We took the meat close to the camp area. We hung that meat up high in a tree and a ways from our siwash. We made sure everything else stayed where I'd gotten the moose.

"We took our turns staying awake through the night watching out in case any bear wanted to join us. We got up early and broke camp. We got the skiff loaded with our gear and the moose meat.

"We got back to the truck and unloaded all the meat. We got the boat on the trailer and we headed to Anchor Town real soon.

"We figured that was the end of the bear story. Nope! We did find out two years later that a hunter had taken the largest brownie ever from the Kenai Peninsula from that exact same area. Right by our camp! We always wondered if it was our bear!

"Well, that's spooky hunting story!" Rich concluded.

Corky shoulders were shaking as she responded, "I'll say it was. That's the second story we've heard today about a bear following a hunter. Those stories make me think twice about traipsing around in the woods."

"It sure reminds me to be careful where there might be a bear," Mark said. "Okay folks! It's time for my bear story as soon as Rich finishes with this wing tank."

"I'll be done here after I wipe it off," Rich said just before he started down the ladder.

Mark grabbed the fuel hose this time as Rich moved the ladder and Corky pulled over a little bit of extra hose so it would reach to the new location at the starboard wing tank.

"When I've started fueling I'll be ready to hear your super bear story Mark," Rich said excitedly.

"It's not a scary one, but I think it's a real neat one, so let me know when you're ready."

"Okay, I'm ready Mark. Go for it."

"So here's my story about the Dandelion bear.

"Seeing a live bear in Alaska is always a thrill and to see one really close is even better.

"I was riding from Anchorage to Anchor Point with a friend. We were driving along the famous Kenai River in the Cooper Landing area with the river on our left side just where the Russian River flows in. There was a guard rail and a little farther along was a group of trees and thick brush. The mountains with their white dots of sheep and goats started rising about a hundred feet off to our right side. It was early summer and lots of salmon were migrating up the Kenai and Russian Rivers into the various streams and lakes.

"Usually at that time of year there would be lots of road traffic, but there wasn't much. It might have been because it was a week day.

"I knew that bears crossed the road to get to the river in this area to catch salmon so I wanted to spot one. Well, I did.

"Up ahead of us and off to the right close to the road was a brown object in a grassy area. It was a big beautiful lightly colored brown bear that didn't seem to be concerned about much. It was on all four legs with an undecided expression on what to do next.

"The driver of the car slowly came to a stop so the bear wouldn't get spooked while I rolled down my window to take some pictures.

"No, I didn't take the window all the way down. I didn't want that bear, or any bear, in my lap!

"We stopped about fifteen feet away from that great creature and I was able to take several shots with the camera. In a few moments it lowered its head and began eating grass. As an omnivore it'll eat meat and different types of plants.

"I wouldn't know until much later just how good those bear pictures would turn out to be. In one of the of the pictures it shows this big bear eating the grass as it was looking straight at me with its set of beady brown eyes!

"And here was the other great surprise! Right in front of the nose of the beady eyed bear was a small bright yellow Dandelion flower!

"What a neat picture!

"That whole experience was just wonderful. It is one of those privileged times to be so close to a wild brown bear and get some great pictures!"

"However, the scene changed quickly as a car pulled in behind us and stopped, causing the bear to look up. And in another few seconds a big semi-truck came rushing down the road and the driver blew its loud air horn. The startled animal backed up a bit before it changed its direction and headed back towards the road and galloped across right in front of us.

"Poof! In a flash the majestic animal was gone as it magically disappeared into the brush!"

"That's an awesome story!" Corky responded as she was smiling and also thinking to herself, *"I wonder who Mark was riding with!"*

Rich was grinning as he added, "That's a neat story Mark. I'd like to see the pictures some day.

"Watching any critter in its natural surroundings is something I really enjoy doing so maybe I'll get to see something like that this summer."

"I hope that you will Rich," Mark stated. "We'll look forward to hearing about your adventures. Be sure to update us when you get back."

Chapter 13   Dane's Encounters

"Okay, let's get Corky's One-charlie over to its spot. And I hear a 206 in the pattern. I wonder if that's Jerry. Did you meet Jerry?" Mark asked Rich.

"Yep. Sure did. I was watching him do his pre-flight check to see if we do it the same way. We do it the same way by always being sure we're paying attention to what we're supposed to be doing.

"Here comes Volts in his truck and I see Donnie's just coming through the hanger door. I think he's headed our way. This has become a might busy place."

Jerry had just made a smooth landing as Don parked his truck by Mark's 206 tie-down spot.

Donnie greeted everybody as he approached the trio at the fuel ramp.

"Hi, folks! Instead of our rolling One-zulu over to its tie-down, let's get it to my hangar. We can get the wheel-skis off and get your big tundra tires put on it.

"When I'm done with that I'll put Corky's Cub One-charlie on wheels and get it down to Beluga Lake and get it on floats. That's what you would like isn't it Corky?"

"Absolutely, Donnie," she replied. "We appreciate the fast service you provide and for understanding what we might need this summer.

"What're your thoughts about Jerry who is just taxing up to Don's truck?"

"Sharp as a tack! Fun! Knows airplanes, but is not a showoff. In fact, I figured you'd keep him so I made another set of keys before I gave your set to him, Mark. The extra set is in my key cabinet."

Mark nodded his head in agreement, "Good thinking Donnie, and thanks.

"While Jerry's passengers are taking a stretch and he and Don are loading up the 206, let's get this puppy to your hangar."

Corky and Mark positioned themselves behind a wing strut to push the airplane while Donnie got just in front of the horizontal stabilizer and next to the fuselage. Now he could move the frame from side to side to guide the plane along as the others did the pushing and pulling.

Rich had finished putting away the fuel equipment so he quickly walked over to help Jerry and Don load Volts' cargo into the plane.

Just as One-zulu was almost to the hanger the big doors started to open. It was a two-part door that was hinged horizontally in the middle. As the lower part was pulled up by cables the door folded in the middle and the folded edge moved out over the ramp. Doug, Donnie's helper, had seen the trio pushing the plane over so he timed the opening to happen just as they arrived.

The trio slowed down when they had the plane inside and past the hanger doors. As it moved under the open door Doug pushed the Close button and the wide doors started closing.

"Okay," Donnie stated out loud. "Let's leave it here. We'll take the skis off after lunch, and then get Eight-one-charlie in here.

"Thanks for helping.

"Doug, do you need me right away to get the skis off this and to get the tundra tires on?"

"I got it Boss. I'm going for a short lunch pretty soon at the Runway Café."

"Sounds good, Doug. We're going over and talk with Jerry Winsmore a bit. I'll see ya at the Café.

"It seems to Doug and me that you two are getting busier. Is that right?" Donnie asked.

As the three were walking to the hangar man-door Mark deferred the answer to Corky. She didn't say a word about the gold diggers as Donnie got an update.

"There are a number of things going coming on soon or that might happen. Flying for Don Volts provides a lot of flying time and we're helping with supplies and support for a group over in the Lake Iliamna area. We want the planes to be ready for any hunting and or sight-seeing trips, cargo runs, and maybe a bear watching trip or too.

"Since my 206 is available at Beluga Lake I want to take it on a test flight and get used to flying it on floats and using that three-bladed propeller," Corky stated.

"So Mark, after we eat lunch do you mind going on that test flight with me? You can check my procedures, and then you fly it and I'll check on yours."

"I'm all for doing that," he answered before he asked Donnie, "Is there anything we need to know other than it has the new three-bladed prop?"

"Nope. It's fueled up and ready to fly. The weight and balance papers are updated, all of the inspections have been completed, and I even cleaned the windshields so you can spot bears easier."

"And speaking of bears, how about that guy and his friends who drove up here from Michigan to see brown bears up close? I'm they sure they got more adventures from their trip than they thought they might get."

"And now another bear story?"

As the three left the hanger and were walking across the pavement over to Four-yankee Donnie started telling what he knew of the bear story.

"Well, this guy who I think was called Dane, and four of his friends drove to Homer from Michigan in a big flat bed truck with a homemade camper on it.

"They charted an Otter on wheels to fly them over to the Hallo Bay area. When they got there and were flying over the river rapids they got real excited about seeing all the brown bears looking for and feeding on the fish.

"But as the roar of the big Otter's radial engine faded away as it flew off, Dane said the reality of how out of touch with the rest of the world they were. He said he felt real small when he thought about how big and remote our Alaska really is."

The trio had reached the other men as Don Volts gave them a wave as he was driving away in his truck.

Jerry he reached out to shake Corky's hand as he stated, "Hi folks. Don forgot a box so he's going back to the shop to get it. He'll be back real soon,"

"Hi, Corky! It's been awhile since we met and thanks for the opportunity to fly with you folks."

"Good to see you Jerry. Glad you can be here and how was the trip to Seldovia?"

"Very interesting for sure. There are a lot of black bears on the other side this Bay.

"I didn't have any trouble finding my way over there or landing. These Volts' gentlemen were ready to go and so we got loaded up real quick like.

"The field hadn't been graded yet so the landing and takeoff were as bumpy as expected.

"Omigosh! That town sure got damaged. These men told me that though the place will never be the same the local folks have a real good attitude about surviving. I tip my hat off to those folks for having such a "we'll make it okay" attitude."

"That is so typical of most Alaskans." Mark stated.

Corky waved for the three other men to come over and join their group. As they arrived she told them that Donnie was just telling a story of some bear watchers he had heard about.

"You fellows might find this story interesting."

Donnie, who was enjoying the attention of having so many listeners, tipped his cap back and looked each of them in the eyes as he retold the first part of the story.

He moved the cap back even farther as he related the rest of the adventure tale.

"So they made a tent camp on the beach way above the high tide mark. Before they headed up to the rapids they saw bears walking on the beach and mud flats not far away from their tent.

"They had just two pistols with them.

"Anyway, over the next several days Dane said they had several very close encounters with the brown bears, the big ones and the small ones.

"Many times a guy would see a bear coming down a path towards him so the guy would quickly get behind a tree, or step off the path. Dane said we need to know that many of the trees weren't as wide as any of the men.

"Fortunately, the brownies weren't bothered by the men and literally walked right next to them while passing by. The bears were so close a guy could've put a hand on its rump, but the bears had their intentions on eating the river fish. They wasn't the least bit bothered by all of them humans.

"And them bears that were full of fish after leaving the rapids? They didn't seem to be at all perturbed by these guys.

"The brown bear moms with a cub or two were the most aggressive bears and only if the Momma thought the cubs were in danger. Dane said he saw the Momma bears fighting off the big male boars if she felt they were too close to her kids.

"Even with the excitement they were all having, some of these guys almost freaking out, they were really happy campers when the Otter finally roared to a beach landing and picked them up.

"They flew back here to Homer and before you knew it they were driving back to Michigan in that big truck."

The group was amazed that not one of the bears had attacked anyone.

"Well, I could have been attacked for the real dumb thing I did with a bear," Rich volunteered.

Since Don hadn't returned yet, the crowd asked Rich to tell them his bear story.

Chapter 14 Naknek Surprise

"Last year after I had met Corky at Igiugig I finished the summer working as a Catch Sampler for Fish and Game in Naknek by Bristol Bay.

"As you may know Bristol Bay is the largest salmon fishery in the world. The millions of fish are caught by a long net that is set out and attached to a boat that drifts with the current. The name for that combination of net and boat is called "drift fishing" and the fishermen are called "drifters". Not like a drifter in the western stories.

"The fish are taken to a cannery sometimes by a tender which is a large boat that can hold thousands of fish that had been collected from the drifters.

"The fish were processed and put into cans at the canneries, thus the name cannery. Those cans of fish are put onto big trays. The trays are put on dollies and rolled into big steam retorts and cooked. Then the dollies are pulled out and the cans get cooled off naturally by the local air. The cans are then put into cardboard cases.

"One of the bigger canneries is on the shore of the Naknek River in a small community called Naknek. The Naknek River flows into Bristol Bay. That cannery can produce thousands of cases of canned fish which are then distributed across the rest of the world.

"To do that processing requires an incredible amount of raw fish. After the fish are processed the backbones and heads sometimes wind up on the River's beaches.

"The brown bears know this, and they go down to the beach by the cannery and scrounge for the fish scraps.

"Within a few hundred feet of the beach there can be twenty bears looking for scraps.

"As I mentioned I was a Catch Sampler for Fish and Game's Commercial Fisheries Research section. After finding out how and where the fish had been caught I'd take some random samples of the whole fish to a work area to gather information about it.

"After I determined the species of the fish, its general condition, size, sex, and weight I recorded the data. I'd then pull off a fish scale from about two-thirds back from the gills. The fish scale would be placed on a small card that had a series of numbers on it to identify each one of the samples. The card had been covered with adhesive material so the fish scales would stay stuck to the paper.

"During the winter a fish scientist would use a high pressure press that made a mold of the scale in a piece of plastic. With the use of a microscope the scale's ring pattern would show that fish's age and growth rate.

"I got off track. So anyway when my job was finished I'd go down to the beach and watch the bears go after the fish scraps. It was neat to observe how they mingled with each other with just an occasional snarl at each other.

"One day a co-worker and I were walking on a path through a bushy area to get to a viewing spot. He was following a ways behind me. As I went around a corner I was suddenly face to face with a brown bear. It was less than four feet away!

"I shrieked and threw my arms up.

"The bear shrieked and stood with its arms up!

"The next thing I knew, I was doing exactly what you shouldn't do: I was running away. When I looked to see if it was behind me, I saw it looking back at me and it was running away!

"The co-worker was laughing so hard he had tears running down his cheeks.

"From then on we used a different route to get to the beach for any bear watching!"

The crowd was hooting and hollering at Rich's story just as Don drove into the parking area. After getting out of the parked truck he asked what was going on.

Rich quickly re-told his story as Don was handing the retrieved cargo box to Jerry. The box had been loaded and secured in Four-yankee as Rich finished his story.

Don was chuckling as he shook his head in disbelief before he stated, "My story is a real short one so I won't be holding Jerry up from getting out of here."

The three man crew wanted to hear their boss' story so they didn't get into the plane.

"My wife, Barb and my kids went out East End Road to Corky's cabin yesterday morning to check on it. On the way out Barb stopped at Jeanine's to find out how well she was surviving the quake and tremors.

"Now Jeanine had been known to chase black bears from her cabin up into the various draws that come down the bluffs out East End road

"It turns out a black bear, maybe it was one she had chased before, may not have been any too happy about being woke up from its winter sleep. That bear got into a storage shed of Jeanine's and had stood on and crushed every cardboard box. That bear had reached up to swipe anything and everything it could get its paws on off of the shelves. Barb and the kids could only find two items that survived that bear's frustration. What a mess!

"Jeanine said she'd clean the place up later, but a big concern is the bear might be back to look for something to eat, or to mess up the shed even more. That would be hard to do, but bears are known to come back to a spot where they hadn't been chased away from.

"Well, it's not much of a story, but it just shows you that a bear can be a real bother even if it isn't bothering you personally!"

"Right on, Don! I know bears can be that way and someday I might tell you about my blackie experience," Jerry said as he shook Volts' hand. "But for now I'm on my way as soon as these men get buckled in."

"Have a great flight Jerry. I do want to hear a good bear story when you get back," Don replied as he waved to his crew.

"It's lunch time. Care to join us at the Runway Café for a bite to eat?" Corky asked Don.

"You betcha I will! Barb is watching the shop and she figured I might be awhile so let's do it. And while we're there Corky, you can tell me a good bear story. It seems to be the trend of the day."

"Compared to some of the stories we've heard today mine will be pretty mild."

Doug was leaving the hangar on his way to lunch so he joined up with the others.

The six were still chattering as they entered the Café and were greeted by the waitress and their friend Marilyn.

"Donnie and Doug are on time for their regular noon meal and he brought along four of our friends. Welcome!

"You folks pull those tables together while I deliver this order to our FAA friend Richard."

All six arrivals flooded Richard with hellos and he gestured for them to pull over the two tables next to his as Marilyn set his order down.

In a few minutes four of the six had placed their orders except Donnie and Doug who just waited for their standard lunch to be served.

Corky pointed out to Richard, "Today is the day for great bear stories so Mark and I have been pleasurably treated to a variety of great tales. Since you've traveled a lot in Alaska I'd bet you have had some interesting bear experiences. Would you care to share?"

"Well, I guess I've had one or two. You folks start and I'll tell mine after I've chowed down some great food and while you're eating lunch."

"Sounds good to me," Don said. "Okay Corky. Let's hear your story."

Chapter 15   Cooper Landing Momma Brown

"It's not going to be as exciting as Rich's or Mark's but here goes.

"One time I was in Anchorage when a woman asked if I'd pick up her son from Ninilchik and fly him back to the big city. I jumped at the chance to be flying a plane so we flew down in a Cessna 172 that I had available.

It has a tricycle gear and metal fuselage. You usually land a tricycle geared aircraft with the nose slightly up so as you land on a gravel field like Ninilchik's, every piece of rock and sand that hits the metal fuselage does so with a loud clank sound. You can really notice it if the back is empty. It can be a disturbing sound even when you know why it occurs.

"So anyway, we left Anchorage's International Airport and picked her son up at Ninilchik. We all decided to take the opportunity to do some sightseeing instead of making a direct trip back to Anchor Town. I had our Plan altered to include legs to Sterling and to the mouth of the Skilak Lake, and then over to the Kenai River, through Cooper Landing to the Kenai Lake and further on to Tern Lake.

"Then we would turn left to fly to the Turnagain Pass area, over to and up the Turnagain Arm and onward to the Anchorage Airport.

"That's a very pretty trip as you get to see the Kenai Burn area that's as flat as can be. Skilak Lake is long and wild with glaciers at the head of it in the Kenai Mountains. Then you see the Kenai River with its white water rapids before it flows into Kenai Lake. Real quick you get into the narrow valleys of the Kenai Mountains.

"We were on the Kenai River's south side at Cooper Landing when we spotted a big brown bear with two cubs leisurely moving along on a high bench on the north side.

"After I checked that there wasn't another aircraft in the area I slowed down and crossed the Kenai to get us closer to the bears.

"By staying high enough above the animals we didn't disturbed them with the engine's noise.

"The animals kept a steady easy pace through the tall grass as they moved up and down the hills.

"Their coats were glossy and all of them looked very healthy. As you know they can eat small and big animals, berries and just about anything else that's available.

Many of those black and brown bears that live high up on the mountainsides are not fish bears, but that's not always the case.

"I've often wondered if those bears we saw had ever taken the long trek down the mountain to the Kenai River to eat any of those migrating salmon."

"We enjoyed the beautiful mountainous country that included lakes and some goats that were up high.

"And we checked out a few of the old hard rock gold mine adits that were almost at a mountain's peak. Those adits were created around the turn of the century by the tough miners of that era.

"There's a few drift mining operations lower down on the Quartz Creek, Sixmile Creek, and Hope areas."

Doug seemed to be listening just a little more intently than he usually did as Corky finished her story. Then he said in his dry manner of speaking, "It's beautiful country. I panned in Canyon Creek and Sixmile area. Didn't get much. I want to go back. Try it again."

When he was finished Doug started sipping coffee as if he hadn't said a word about anything.

"That's the same place Jeff Budny, the assayer, told us that when he was a kid, his friend, John, picked a gold nugget out of the creek with chewing gum and a stick."

"It is a beautiful place alright," Donnie agreed before he added. I've been through there many times. If you got to drive it in the winter, be real careful. The two-lane road from Turnagain Arm up into Turnagain Pass can be slick.

"In fact, that entire road from Anchorage to Homer is dangerous, what with its sharp curves, icy roads, moose and porcupine almost leaping out of the bushes to get in front of you. Sometimes the snow's so deep the moose can't or won't get off the road. You have to slow down at times almost to a stop to be sure you don't hit the big or little animals."

"When does a Porky ever leap out of the bushes?" Rich asked.

"Whenever a bear is after it!" Richard answered.

The crowd in the Runway Café went wild with jeers and cheers just as Marilyn arrived with the first orders of lunch. When she heard Richard's answer she began to laugh so hard she almost dropped the plates of food.

Don Volts was setting his cup down when he started talking about his bear story, "When we came down the Sterling Highway it was still gravel and had lots and lots of sharp turns.

"When you got through the Cooper Landing area and you were about to cross the Kenai River just a few miles below Cooper Creek, you would be going around a sharp corner and 'Pow' there was a wooden covered bridge!

"Anybody remember that bridge?"

Everyone at the table and a few of the customers at the counter responded with "Oh yeahs", and "Yeps".

"Well, not too far upriver from that old bridge site I stopped at a curve pullout and watched a medium-sized brownie for awhile. It was walking along a gravel bar on the far shore. I noticed it would pull up something for a moment, and then drop it and walk along until it did the same thing again. I looked closely and realized it was checking the river's beach for fish carcasses.

"I did get some pictures of it sniffing the beach, but other than that they were too fuzzy to print out. The bear looked to be in good shape so I figured it must have been eating okay up to then. It didn't seem to be in a hurry to be dining on any of those fish carcasses."

Chapter 16   Glacier Bay's Black Bears

Donnie set his coffee cup down a little harder than usual before he looked around to see if anybody was paying him any attention. When he realized they were he started talking.

"I didn't realize how many bears there were in the Glacier Bay and Gustavus area in Southeastern Alaska. At the time I was there on a tour boat the salmon were running in the creeks and the bears were feasting real well. I saw several black bears walking on the beaches searching for carcasses, clams, fish, or anything else they could eat. Every black bear was big and it wore a glossy coat.

"When our tour boat, a small one compared to some of the others, got close to the glaciers we spotted lots of seals floating on the ice bergs. The tour guide said they were about to pup which meant that new baby seals were going to be born any day!

"That also meant that if the seal pup didn't survive it might wind up on a beach where a bear might find it.

"Nature has a way of keeping its own balance and sometimes not to our personal liking, but we are also a part of nature."

"I agree," Richard stated. "One time when I was in Seward I heard about a stranded black bear cub. It was up in the parking lot where the Resurrection Creek goes into the tunnel before it dumps into Resurrection Bay. I went up to check it out. When I got there I heard a few people wanting to keep the bear cub and others said it belonged with its mom.

"The Momma black bear couldn't be seen but she was snapping her teeth and growling. People didn't know if they should pick up the cub and place it close to the Momma, or just what to do. Someone finally called the Fish and Game office for some help.

"One of their guys went to the parking lot and sized up what was going on. After he put on some new gloves he picked up the little guy who wasn't bigger than a pup. That fellow held the cub as far away from his shirt as he could to keep any human smell off the cub. Then he very slowly carried the little guy over to the thick brushy area where Momma was still making noise. The cub was set down as close to the Alders as the guy felt he could.

"As he slowly backed away the Momma quit clacking her teeth, but it seemed to be making some kind of talk with the cub. The cub got up and walked into the brush.

The crowd was silent. Then Momma gave out a loud sniff and off into the hillside the two went."

As the folks in the café discussed the values of letting Nature run its course, or to intervene in a natural process Marilyn arrived with the rest of the lunches.

As she set them in front of the table diners she loudly announced for everyone to hear which included the folks sitting at the counter, "Okay folks! Bubba and I want to hear Corky's next story. I know she'll have one because she and her family probably have had more Alaskan experiences than most folks ever thought of having.

"If I hear even a peep from anybody until she's ready to talk they'll have to pay everyone else's lunch bill!"

Immediately the place went silent, but everyone was grinning and trying not to chuckle or make any noise.

Corky, whose face had turned red, glanced at Mark who was sitting next to her. He was trying so hard to keep from laughing he was about to choke. She gently hit is right leg with her left one as if to say, "I'll get you later!"
    Everyone quietly and quickly ate their lunches. At last Corky raised both of her hands and announced she had finished eating.
    There was some happy pounding on the counter and a series of yahoos in various forms from everyone before they turned to face Corky.
    "I hope you find this interesting, but I'll get over by the door before I start," she said while starting to get up.
    "Won't happen," Lee, the new Postmaster, stated as he quickly went to the ramp door to block her way out while Bubba stood at the front door.
    "Okay, you folks asked for it so here goes!"

Chapter 17 Klawock River

"When you two mentioned fish carcasses Don and Donnie, I thought of my parents experiences when they were at Klawock on the Prince of Wales Island. It's west of Ketchikan and accessible only by ferry boat or plane. Once you get there you can drive over a lot of the island. It's a very beautiful area and quite wet from all of the rain.

"Fish are an important part of the life of Southeastern Alaska, which is also called the Panhandle. Not only are there drifters, but there are trollers and trawlers, seiners, subsistence users, sport fishermen, and the occasional fish hatchery.

"And of course there are bears. Lots of bears! Brown bears and black bears, Glacier bears and bears with odd colorations, but no Polar bears, or Panda bears!

The Runway Café crowd grunted in response to her bit of bear humor.

"At the south end of the Prince of Wales Island at a small Tlingit community there is a unique fish hatchery. It's unique because not only is it the second oldest one in the state, it uses the Klawock Lake water to raise the fish. The fish are therefore always exposed to the same water and get a solid imprint of its chemistry.

"The return runs of the various fish species are quite strong and healthy with some of the largest Silver salmon in the world in those returns.

"During the spring and summer seasons the various fish species migrate up the Klawock River by the many thousands. The fish include the Kings or Chinooks, the Silvers or Cohos, the Reds or Sockeyes, the Pinks or Humpies, the Chums or Dogs, and even the Steelheads.

"People from all over the world travel there to fish the Klawock River from its mouth to the weir. The stretch of fishable river is only about a mile and half long, but it can be packed from bank to bank with migrating salmon.

"So if you want to see black bears then Klawock is your place. There are lots and lots of black bears feeding on the thousands of fish that swim up the Klawock River.

"The Klawock Lake water is diverted into a spillway for the fish to swim up and into a holding pool. That lake water is used in the hatchery in the fish tanks where the fish's fertilized eggs mature to Fry that are transported using the lake water up to the holding and feeding pens way up in the lake away from the lake's outlet.

"There's a weir that stretches at an angle across the river just below the hatchery and the Klawock Falls. The fish are diverted by the weir into a channel of the rushing lake water so the fish swim up that channel onto a wet sorting deck. Those fish that are to be sold to raise the money for the hatchery are slid across a wet deck into a holding pool.

"The other fish are hustled into the water channel to swim back into the river just below the natural falls.

"So now the fish have to battle the black bears at the Klawock River Falls before they can swim up and into Klawock Lake. Once there the fish migrate through the lake into the various feeder streams to spawn where the stream black bears, and I'm told some brownies, can eat an awful lot of the spawning fish.

"At the peak of the fish runs there are so many black bears at the Falls it can get very crowded with both adult and immature bears.

"Sometimes you could see several black bears trying to catch a jumping fish or a fish that was working hard to swim up the rapids.

"This is where I was going to start.

"Those black bears can be so numerous during the salmon runs that the people who live on the hatchery's property, have to peek out a window to be sure a bear isn't by the door or so close that it could keep someone from leaving.

"One of the bear trails from the forested area to the Falls is right next to the porch of a worker's residence. I do mean immediately next to the porch deck. He always has to look to see if a bear was coming by to get to the Falls or was ready to go back up the trail.

"The hatchery employees were always alert to watch out for the black bears. Many times the folks going to or from the boat launch at the lake and the hatchery had to stop to wait for a bear and sometimes several bears and cubs, to cross over the narrow dirt access road.

"One time there was a Momma black bear sow with three tiny cubs. Very small cubs! Not much bigger than the size of a kid's small Teddy bear.

"One of the triplets was crippled and walked with a limp and usually lagged behind the rest of the family. That kept Momma in a pretty grumpy mood.

"You don't want to argue with a grumpy Momma: bear or no bear!

Several sounds of agreement burbled from Corky's very attentive audience, and then everyone was silent as they waited for her to continue.

"While Momma was out of sight hiding in the brush and the trees between the road and the Falls she'd talk to the cub. With grunts, sighs, grunts, mumbles, and more grunts the little one finally limped across the road in front of the workers.

"No one moved until they knew for sure that Momma had moved her three cubs to the rapids.

"Now the bears would also fatten up by getting to the fish that had spawned out upstream and washed down against the weir. Even the fish that got too weak to jump or swim upriver would float down against that weir. Those spent carcasses, whether they were in the lake or in the river, added nutrients to the whole water system.

"If you walked across the weir towards the far river bank you could hear the bears moving around in the brush. They didn't want to leave the fish bounty, and they also didn't want any humans to be messing with their fish.

"To remove the piled up fish the hatchery guys poked a pew stick into the dead fish. Then it would be flipped up and over the weir to continue floating down the river. As the fish were being flipped away the fish the guys had to keep talking out loud to keep the bears from getting onto the weir from the far side.

"That pew stick they used was essentially a curved nail at the end of a long wooden handle. The pew sticks have always been a part of Alaska's fishing industry, but I've never heard of a pew being able to fend off a bear. End of story."

The crowd went wild with applause and cheers not only for the appreciation of Corky's story, but for the great time everyone had from hearing so many bear stories.

"Well, its time for Doug and I to get back to work," Donnie said reluctantly as he got up from the table.

"It sure is Donnie," Corky responded as she and Mark slid out of their chairs and headed to the cash register.

"We're going to Beluga Lake now and test fly my 206 with that new propeller," Corky commented before she added, "And maybe we'll get to see some more bears!"

Glossary: People, Alaskan places, misc.
(The pronunciations are approximations!)

<u>Alisha and Charlie</u>: Athabaskan Nondalton residents

<u>Anchorage aka Anchor Town</u>: The largest city in Alaska located at the juncture of Turnagain Arm, Knik Arm and Cook Inlet in Southcentral Alaska. It is the major business, military, and population center of Alaska.

<u>Bobby Randall</u>: Homer auto mechanic.

<u>Brown or grizzly bear</u>: Basically the same bear species with some regional differences. Bears living away from the coast are typically called grizzlies, and brownies are by the coast. The names are interchanged by most people.

<u>Brenda Randall</u>: Bobby's sister

<u>Bush Alaska</u>: The name for off-the-road locations.

<u>Carver</u>: Joshua Barrie's nickname: a former refueler in Iliamna; the son of John Barrie.

<u>Donnie</u>: A Homer aircraft mechanic.

<u>Don and Barb Volts</u>: Owners of Volts' Electric in Homer.

<u>Doug</u>: Donnie's helper.

<u>FBO</u>: Fixed Base Operator, a supplier of fuel and aviation maintenance.

<u>Gold</u>: A valuable mineral found as flakes, nuggets or in veins of quartz rocks. It can be a good item for some folks and a tribulation for others.

<u>Harry Pridgetti</u>: FBO and aircraft charter operator in Bethel in Southwest Alaska.

<u>Homer</u>: A small fishing and farming community on Kachemak Bay on the Kenai Peninsula in Southcentral Alaska.

<u>Kenai Peninsula</u>: A Southcentral Alaska peninsula that is bigger than almost any other U.S. State.

<u>Iliamna</u>: (ill ee amna) An airport area in Southwest Alaska by Lake Iliamna and west of the Alaska Range of mountains.

Jeff Budny: Alaskan assayer; Mathew's dad.
Jerry Winsmore: A former grocery clerk and now a pilot.
John Barrie: An Iliamna fuel vendor.
Kachemak Bay: (catch eh mack) A deep estuary bay on the south end of the Kenai Peninsula.
Lake Iliamna: The eighth largest freshwater lake in the USA and home to freshwater seals.
Lucinda Miranda: Former Homer Postmaster & spinster.
Merrill Field: A small airfield in Anchorage for land based general aviation.
Muskeg: A spongy combination of moss, plants, dirt, and water that can be waist deep and very difficult to walk over or through. The mosquito's a sucking bug, and the "No-see-um" biting bugs and other bugs thrive in muskeg areas.
Nikolaevsk: (nick ol lye efsk) An Old Believer's village seven miles east of Anchor Pt. & twenty-three miles north of Homer.
Nondalton: An Athabaskan village at Six Mile Lake a few miles north of Iliamna.
Pam: Niece to Alisha and Charlie. A Nondalton native who is a refueler at Barrie's FOB in Iliamna
Poke: A leather bag or pouch with a drawstring used to carry gold. Small pokes held about a teaspoon of gold and a large one could hold over a quart of gold.
Paula Randall: The mother of Bobby and Brenda.
Old Believers: Old Russian Orthodoxy followers who refused Tsarist controls to emigrate to many places around the world.
Ralph Baring: Corky's Anchorage lawyer.
Rich Williamson: A former Fish & Game tech.; aircraft refueler.
Richard Downing: "Homer Radio" FSS operator.
Runway Café: A small café at the Homer Airport.
Seldovia: Russian for herring. Once a Tsarist Russian herring harvesting site; later a major Cook Inlet fishing town.

Seward: An ice-free seaport of Resurrection Bay.

Short-talk: An abbreviated form of speaking.

Siwash: A temporary camp using a cover piece of material for shelter from rain and wind; usually built next to a small fire.

Spasiba: (spah see bah) Russian for "Thank you!"

Tall Man: Cora's husband, Alexi.

Tavarisch: (tah vahr ish) Russian for "friend".

Tina: Marian's sister in Iliamna

Tremor: the shaking of the land by an earthquake.

Tundra: A wet area of plant covered permafrost. It is very difficult to walk through. It is a major habitat resource for the nesting areas used by thousands of migrant birds.

Tussocks: Small hillocks of plants and dirt that can't be walked on by any animal without a real good possibility of a sprain or injury to the foot, ankle, leg, hip, and/or muscles.

Volts' Electric: See Don Volts'

Vash privetstvuyetsya: (vawsh preevets voo eestyah) Russian "You're welcome."

Wilco: "Will comply with your request."

Enjoy your Journey!
Email: billofalaska@hotmail.com
POB 1325 Anchor Point, AK 99556
www.billofalaska.com